KU-208-531

Contents

CHAPTER		PAGE
1.	THE DANCER	1
2.	QUASIMODO	7
3.	DANGEROUS STREETS	16
4.	THE BROKEN CUP	23
5.	THE MARRIAGE NIGHT	31
6.	THE PILLORY	38
7.	SPELLING THE SECRET	45
8.	FROLLO ASKS QUESTIONS	51
9.	THE CAPTAIN AND THE GIRLS	57
10.	AT THE HOUSE BY THE RIVER	60
11.	THE TRIAL	67
12.	TORTURE	73
13.	A WAY OF ESCAPE	76
14.	THE ROPE	79
15.	ABOVE THE CITY	87
16.	THE PLAN OF ATTACK	92
17.	NOISES IN THE NIGHT	98
18.	THE LOST AND FOUND	106
	QUESTIONS	115
	EXTRA WORDS	122

One

THE DANCER

"I'm cold and I'm hungry," said Pierre Gringoire, "and I haven't any money to buy my supper. No one wants the poems and the plays that I've written, and no one wants me."

Paris, twelve days after Christmas in the year 1482, was a cold city; and many people who lived there were as cold, poor and thin as the poet Pierre Gringoire.

"I must give up being a writer," he said, "I shall die of hunger if I do not." He pushed his hands into his empty pockets and walked towards the square called the Place de Grève. "Look at that crowd! They seem to be warm enough; I'll join them round their fire."

Many men and women were standing in the middle of the square. They looked black against the red light of a big fire of wood burning on the stones. Gringoire hurried across. There seemed to be a large open space between the people and the fire.

"I'm freezing!" said Gringoire, pushing into the crowd. "Why don't we all move nearer to the fire?"

"Because we must leave room for Esmeralda, of course!" replied a fat fellow beside him.

"Who? I've never heard . . ."

"Well, use your eyes. Look at her; isn't she lovely?"

1

Gringoire made himself tall enough to see over the hat of the woman in front of him, and then he understood. There was Esmeralda! She was dancing between the watching crowd and the bright fire.

Gringoire, the poet, was not sure at first whether the graceful dancer was a girl or a fairy! She was small, with a dark skin and black hair. Her eyes were black too, and they shone as she danced. Her little feet moved on a rich Persian cloth which she had thrown over the stones of the square. Her dress was of many colours, bright with gold. Her legs and her shoulders were beautiful. In her right hand she carried a little drum with bells on it, and she hit it as she danced round and round.

"No," Gringoire said aloud, "she's not a fairy; I've seen *gipsies* with hair and eyes like those—but not as beautiful!"

"Of course she's a gipsy," said the fat fellow. "She's one of those wandering people who live in tents and move about from place to place, and she knows all the gipsies' tricks. . . . See there!"

Esmeralda picked up two swords from the ground, and made them stand on their points on her head. Then she danced round one way, while the swords went the other way. The red light from the fire added magic to her trick, and the crowd watched and wondered in silence.

"I could write a poem about this," thought Gringoire. He looked across the fire, at the corner of the square where the terrible *gibbet* stood. Many men and women had hung by the neck from that wooden arm. Gringoire felt suddenly afraid. "But why am I afraid?" he wondered; "I haven't broken the law."

Then he looked at the other corner of the square, at the little building called the Rat-Hole. Sister Gudule lived in the Rat-Hole, in one room with iron bars across its only window. She could never come out: the Rat-Hole had no door. Everyone knew that she hated gipsies. She could not have seen Esmeralda, or she would have shouted curses, as she always did when gipsies came into the Place de Grève.

Esmeralda danced faster and faster, and the eyes of one face in the crowd around Gringoire were fixed on her with a strange look. The face was calm and still; but the eyes burned. The man was not more than thirty-five years old, but there were only a few hairs left on his head, and they were grey. Gringoire could see only his head: the man's clothes were hidden by the crowd.

The girl, breathless, stopped dancing, and the crowd shouted for more.

"Djali!" cried Esmeralda.

Gringoire then saw a little white goat come up to her. Its feet were golden, and it wore a silver chain round its neck. Gringoire had not noticed the goat before, because it had been lying down to watch Esmeralda dance.

"Djali," she said, "now it's your turn." She sat down and held out her drum to the goat.

"Djali," she asked, "what day of the month is it?"

The goat lifted its foot and, to the delight of the people, hit the drum six times.

"Well done, Djali!" shouted the children in the front of the crowd.

"What a wonderful beast!" cried the fat fellow.

"Djali," said the gipsy, moving the drum round a little, "which hour of the day is it?"

Djali lifted a gold foot and hit the drum seven times. At that moment the clock in the tower beside the square struck seven.

"It is all done by black magic," said an evil voice in the crowd. It was the voice of the man whose eyes were always on the gipsy girl. She turned round quickly, but the crowd shouted and the shouts hid the man's words.

"Djali," said the girl to please the crowd, "how do priests speak to people in church?"

The goat sat down and began to make a silly noise, waving its front feet in the air in a funny way. The people laughed and shouted as loud as they could.

"It is wrong! It is bad!" cried the voice of the man with only a few grey hairs.

The gipsy turned round again.

"Oh!" she said, "it's that ugly man!" and she put out her tongue at him. But there was fear in her eyes as she turned from him and went round among the crowd to collect money on her drum.

The people were generous, and when she came to Gringoire her drum was covered with big and little coins of gold and silver. Without thinking, Gringoire put his hand in his pocket. Of course he found that it was empty. "The Devil!" said Gringoire, feeling hot and foolish while the pretty girl stood in front of him with her drum. She watched him with her beautiful eyes, while he felt more and more silly. If he had been rich, he would have given all his wealth to her!

A voice saved him, the voice of a woman from the far corner of the square.

"Go away! Bad girl! Gipsy!" cried the voice of the holy woman from the Rat-Hole.

This voice, which frightened Esmeralda, pleased the children and made them laugh.

"It's Sister Gudule!" they shouted. "Hasn't she had her supper? She must be hungry! We'll find her some food!" And they ran away.

That made Gringoire remember how hungry he was and wonder where he would find any supper himself.

"Poor Sister Gudule!" said the fat fellow beside him. "She doesn't have much fun. I wonder what sorrow made her leave the world and go to live a holy life in the Rat-Hole."

"Don't you know her story?" asked Gringoire. "I thought everybody in Paris knew that."

"Of course I know the story that her baby daughter was stolen by gipsies, but I don't believe one word of it. Poor old Sister Gudule is far too ugly ever to have a child worth stealing."

"Sorrow has made her ugly," said Gringoire. "I can believe that she was beautiful sixteen years ago, when the gipsies changed her baby for a boy who was four years old."

"A boy with only one eye, and arms and legs all the wrong shape. I know that story, but I still don't believe that Sister Gudule . . ."

"Haven't you seen the little baby's shoe in her Rat-Hole? And haven't you seen her weeping over it? Her heart is broken. If you had any poetry in you, you would understand that the story fits the facts."

"Poetry!" he laughed. "You'll tell me next that you're a poet yourself!"

Gringoire said nothing, because he heard the music of a strange but very sweet song. Esmeralda was singing it. The words, in the gipsy language, were full of joy, and her voice was as bright and pure as that of a bird.

The children had gone to find some food for Sister Gudule; they came back from a dark, narrow street into the square. The biggest girl carried a cake. They came to the front of the crowd and stood there, listening to the wonderful song. The children were hungry too; they broke pieces off the cake and ate them while they listened to Esmeralda singing.

The music did not last long.

From the Rat-Hole came another ugly shout in Sister Gudule's voice. "Won't you be silent? Won't you stop that noise and let us have some peace?"

The song stopped suddenly. "You have broken the loveliest music I ever heard!" Gringoire cried.

The people were angry too, and shouted. Some of them called:

"The Devil take Sister Gudule!" and, as they

ugly big head sunk down below his shoulders, and his thick arms and legs all the wrong shape. But now the crowd wanted him. He did not know why: he could not understand because he could hear nothing. The drums of his big ears had been broken by the noise of the bells which he rang every day in the church of Notre-Dame. He loved his bells, although he could not hear them until they made their loudest music. He could only feel them ringing, and the bells pleased him more than anything in his sad life.

Gilles Clopin, a nasty young man, danced up the steps of the church and stood like Quasimodo, with his head down below his shoulders. He made a rude face at Quasimodo. Although the hunchback could not hear, he could see with one eye. Clopin was making fun of him, and the hunchback was angry. The crowd laughed, but the hunchback did not. He stepped quickly to Clopin, picked up the young man in his strong, ugly hands, lifted him high into the air as if Clopin were as light as a baby, and threw him down the steps.

The people were silent; then they shouted more loudly than ever: but most of the women felt afraid of Quasimodo.

"He's as ugly as a monkey!" said one woman.

"And as evil as he is ugly!" said another.

"I live near Notre-Dame, and I hear him running about on the roof all night long."

"Like a cat."

"If you're going to have a baby, Louise, keep away from the hunchback," said a grandmother.

"He's really terrible."

But the men were pleased with the hunchback, and they laughed and shouted when they saw his strength. The beggars in the crowd brought a crown of paper and a length of bright, painted cloth. They put the crown on Quasimodo's head and hung the cloth over his ugly body. Then they pushed a big cross of rough wood into his hands. They lifted him onto an old door which they had broken down, and carried him through the city with ugly music, songs and laughter. "Quasimodo!" they shouted, "High Priest Quasimodo! Make way for the High Priest of Fools!"

Sixteen years before the beginning of this story, on a fine day in spring, a child was found after the morning service in the church of Notre-Dame. He was lying on a step. His body was covered with a dirty old cloth, and he was crying in a strange way.

Little babies, whom their mothers did not want, were often left at that place in the church: kind women took them away and cared for them as if the children were their own. But this little boy was already four years old; he had red hair, only one eye, and a body all the wrong shape. Nobody wanted this child.

Some women stood looking at him.

"What can it be?" asked one.

"God help us if that is how babies are born now!" said another.

"Let me see! I can't see!" cried a pretty little girl in lovely clothes.

"No, Fleur dear, it's not nice, it's not at all nice,

come away this minute!" and Fleur's rich mother pulled her away by the hand.

The little baby boy wept loudly. He did not cry like other children.

"I think it's a magic animal, not a boy at all," said a frightened old woman. "A bad magician has made it."

"You're right," said another. "It's a strange, evil animal."

A man stood behind the women and listened to their talk. He was young Claude Frollo, an important priest in the church of Notre-Dame, and already one of the most learnéd men in Paris. People were afraid of his serious face, and some even whispered that he was so clever he knew how to do magic. When the women noticed Frollo they hurried away.

Frollo stood looking at the little boy, and his heart filled with pity. "No woman wants you, child, because you are different from other children," he thought. "But God made you, and God wants everybody whom He has made. We must love the ugly people as well as the beautiful ones, just as He does. Come to me, poor boy!"

Frollo picked the child up in his arms, and it stopped crying. The priest felt suddenly at peace. He knew that he was doing what God wanted him to do.

"I will take care of you, my boy," said Frollo. "Now you belong to me, my child. Come." He walked through the church with the child in his arms.

Frollo named the little boy Quasimodo. Quasimodo had only one eye, but there was nothing wrong with his ears at first. He could speak, too, but not as clearly as he could hear. His voice was rough and strange. Frollo tried to teach him to speak better, and the child worked very hard to improve. But Quasimodo's body was so ugly that he did not want other people to see him. He ran away from men and women and other children, and hid in the tower of the church. He would stay with Frollo, but with no one else. Frollo cared for him and taught him to ring the bells of Notre-Dame.

The bells ruined his ears, and made them *deaf*, so that he could not hear anything: then Quasimodo stopped speaking. He was too afraid of other people to let them hear his strange voice. If he spoke they might laugh. Frollo had tried to set Quasimodo's tongue free, but Quasimodo made it silent.

Although he could not speak with his own tongue, the hunchback could speak to the whole of Paris through the bells of Notre-Dame. He loved everything in that beautiful church, but he loved the bells most of all, especially the great bell named Marie. Marie hung in the south tower, with a small bell called Jacqueline. In the second tower there were six other bells; and the six smallest were in the centre tower, with the wooden bell that was only rung when people died. So Quasimodo had fifteen bells to love. But Marie was his favourite.

Quasimodo's joy when he could ring all the bells on special days was wonderful. He and Frollo spoke together by strange signs. As soon as Frollo told the hunchback that he could start the bells, Quasimodo rushed up the stairs quicker than any other man could run down. He hurried into the room of the great bell, and touched Marie with his hands as if she were a good horse setting out on a long journey. He pitied her for the work that she was about to do.

Then he made a sign to the men down below who pulled the ropes. The first sound of the metal tongue made the floor on which Quasimodo stood shake like a leaf in a storm. Quasimodo shook with the bell. His breath came louder and quicker as the bell rang faster. His one eye opened wide, and seemed to shine with a light of its own in the dark tower.

Then all the bells began to ring and the whole tower shook, stone and wood and metal together, from the top to the bottom. Quasimodo seemed to go mad. He ran from bell to bell, and laughed at the great noise, which was almost the only noise that his ears could hear. Then he stood beside a little bell, and jumped up and down as it swung. At last he left it: he ran to Marie, jumped into the air and hung onto the bell with his feet and his hands. He felt as if he were riding on the clouds of a storm, as he did in his dreams.

The people of Paris often stopped in the streets and listened to the wonderful music of the bells. When it was all finished, Quasimodo came down to Frollo and they talked to each other with the signs which only they knew.

Now Quasimodo, High Priest of Fools, was

being carried into the Place de Grève. He felt as happy as if he were up in the tower and Marie was ringing. He swung on the shoulders of the crowd with his paper crown on his head, and painted cloth over his back, and the cross in his hands. He laughed as he saw more people coming across the square towards him.

One man ran in front of the rest, a man with a few grey hairs and the black clothes of a priest. It was he who had watched Esmeralda so strangely and had shouted at her. Now he came close enough for Quasimodo's one eye to see it was—Frollo; and he saw that Frollo was angry.

Quasimodo jumped from the shoulders which carried him. He rushed to his master, Frollo, and fell on his knees in front of him. Frollo pulled the crown from Quasimodo's head, tore the painted cloth from his back, and broke the wooden cross. Quasimodo stayed on his knees. Then the crowd saw the two making strange signs to each other; the priest was angry and giving orders, the hunchback was sad and asking for mercy. Yet the hunchback, if he had wished, could have thrown the priest across the square with one hand!

At last Frollo shook Quasimodo's strong shoulders, made a sign for him to rise and follow. They turned away.

The crowd was angry at the loss of its High Priest of Fools, and came round Frollo, shouting at him; but Quasimodo was too quick for them. He ran in front of Frollo and stood with his great hands out, ready to hurt any person who came near. Then the

Quasimodo the hunchback fell on his knees in front of Frollo

priest walked slowly out of the square. Quasimodo, making cries like an angry beast, followed through the crowd, and the people were too frightened to touch either of them.

Three

DANGEROUS STREETS

"All this is very strange," Gringoire said to himself; "but where the devil shall I find a supper?"

The crowds were leaving the square, puzzled by the way their High Priest of Fools had gone away from them. People were talking in angry voices as they walked past Gringoire on their way to their homes or to inns.

"Lucky people!" thought Gringoire. "They know where they can get food and drink and a warm bed. But the night will be very hard for me, without a penny in my pocket. Who knows where I can go, so that I may not die of hunger and cold?"

The people took no notice of him, but went away. The fire had nearly died. As Gringoire was leaving the dark, empty square he saw Esmeralda and her little goat walking down a narrow street in front of him.

"She must have a home to go to," thought Gringoire as he began to follow Esmeralda; "and gipsy women's hearts are kind. Perhaps she will lead me to a warm place." He walked faster as she disappeared round a corner. "I'll see where she is going!"

An old man stepped into the brightly lit doorway

of an inn, but Gringoire hurried past him. Gringoire heard happy people inside laughing and singing. Then the door shut, and the street was dark and
silent except for the noise of his own quick steps.
He ran to the corner, and saw the girl and the goat
walking in front of him again. They did not turn
round. Gringoire walked slowly so that she might
not notice that he was following them.

They went on and on. The night became darker
and darker. In the many cold, black streets they
passed only two poor men. Esmeralda and Djali went
down narrow little streets which turned this way and
that way. Gringoire soon had no idea where he was.

Then Esmeralda turned a corner and went
down into a street which was not as dark as the
others. When Gringoire turned into it, he found that
she was waiting beside the bright window of a shop
where bread was being made for the next morning.
She must have heard his steps and wanted to see who
he was. Without a word she looked up at him. She
smiled a little, with pity on her beautiful face: she
knew that he was too weak to do her any harm. Then
she walked on quickly down the empty street. Her
little goat danced happily beside her and its golden
feet glimmered on the stones.

Gringoire felt very foolish; his face was red in the
light from the window. He stood until Esmeralda
turned to the right at the end of the street, and then
he slowly followed her.

As he came to the corner he heard a shout of fear.
It was Esmeralda's voice. Gringoire rushed to her.

The street was filled with deep shadows, but at the far end a little lamp shone. The flame of oil in an iron cage burned as a gift to Our Lady, the mother of Jesus, whose shape, cut out of stone, stood above it. By the light, Gringoire was able to see Esmeralda: she was struggling in the arms of two men. One of the men was dressed in black. They tried to stop her shouts, while the poor little goat, in great alarm, put down its head and cried.

"Help! Help!" shouted Gringoire. "Come, soldiers of the watch, come and help!"

One of the two men, who had taken hold of Esmeralda, turned towards him. The man had only one eye, and his face was very ugly. He was Quasimodo!

Gringoire did not run away; but he did not move a step closer.

Quasimodo ran at him, and threw him onto the stones with one blow of the back of his hand. Then Quasimodo picked up the girl, and carried her away as easily as if she were a feather: they disappeared into the dark. The other man followed them.

"Murder! Murder!" cried the gipsy.

The little goat ran away.

All at once, in a deep voice like the sound of a big gun, came the shout of a man on a horse.

"Stand there! Let the woman go!"

It was a captain of the king's soldiers: he had suddenly appeared from the next road. He was armed from head to foot, and held a long sword in his hand.

He took the gipsy from the arms of the surprised hunchback, and laid her across his horse in front of him. Quasimodo rushed at him to take Esmeralda away, but fifteen or sixteen soldiers, each with a drawn sword, appeared behind their leader. The soldiers made a circle round Quasimodo, seized him and held him. He shouted and fought and bit: they would not let him go. But the man in black ran away and disappeared up the street.

Esmeralda sat in front of the captain on his big horse. She put her hands on the young man's shoulders and looked into his fine face. Then, with a smile, she asked him:

"Captain, what is your name?"

"Captain Phoebus, at your service, my pretty one," said the officer, drawing himself up.

"Thank you," she said. "Thank you, dear Captain."

While Captain Phoebus touched his little beard with pride, she dropped from his horse and fled into the dark.

"By the devil's foot!" cried the captain, as he tied the ropes on Quasimodo with a firmer knot and looked at his ugly face, "I'd rather have kept the girl!"

Gringoire lay on the street under the little lamp. He could not remember how he came there, and as he looked up at the stone feet of Our Lady his head felt as if the figure of Our Lady was going round and round very fast.

"What happened?" he wondered. "And what's this, freezing on my back?"

He touched his clothes. They were wet with the dirty, cold water of the street.

"This is a very nasty place to stay on such a cold night!" He began to get to his feet . . . but he moved slowly, because his head still felt funny; it seemed to be going round the other way now. He lay down again.

Then he heard boys shouting at the tops of their voices:

"Michel's dead! Michel's dead! The old beggar is dead! We'll burn his dirty old bed in front of Our Lady!"

Gringoire felt something soft fall on top of him.

"This is too heavy," thought Gringoire, "and it smells bad." The children had not seen him lying on the road; one of them lit a piece of cloth at the lamp below the feet of Our Lady, to set fire to the bed which they had thrown down.

"I smell burning! . . . yes, it's smoke! . . . I shall be cooked if I stay here!" thought Gringoire. "Help!" he shouted. He struggled out from under the bed, picked it up, threw it at the boys and ran down the street as quick as he could.

"It's the beggar's ghost!" cried the boys. "Save us!" They ran off the other way.

Gringoire went from one street to another with no idea where he was going. At last he stood, resting his back against a house, with his mouth wide open to drink the cold night air.

"What a fool I am!" he thought. "I shouldn't have run away from the boys. They were as afraid of me as I was afraid of them! I should have stayed, and either warmed myself by the fire which they were making, or—if the boys had gone and I could have put out the fire—the old bed would have been mine and I could have slept in it with comfort! I must hurry back!"

He turned round, and went up the dark street. He hurried on and on, often turning to left and right— all the wrong way—until he came into a street where something was burning.

"That's it!" he cried, "that's my bed!" and he began to run.

"Spare a coin for a poor old beggar!" said an ugly voice beside him; and Gringoire saw a creature without any legs coming towards him out of the dark.

"I'm sorry," said Gringoire, "I haven't a penny for myself."

"Spare a little coin, just one little coin!" The beggar without legs pulled himself by sticks along the stones behind Gringoire.

"Give me something, master!" cried another rough voice, and a second beggar appeared, pulling himself along with the help of a stick.

"I tell you I have nothing, my poor friend," Gringoire said.

Then a third beggar rose up in front of him. He was a little blind man, with a long black beard, a white stick, and a big, rough dog to lead him.

"Money, for the love of God!" whispered the blind beggar in a weak voice.

"I have nothing, nothing!" cried Gringoire. The three beggars followed him: he began to feel afraid. They were still following. "I can give you nothing, my poor friends. Please leave me alone!" He started to run down the street.

The beggars followed, and to Gringoire's surprise they followed quickly. The two men without legs threw their sticks aside and showed that they had real strong legs after all! The blind man could see perfectly, and ran faster than his great dog! They all raced along after Gringoire. They came closer and closer. Gringoire shook with fear so that his legs could hardly carry him.

Suddenly he found that he was in a big square. There were many fires burning on the stones. There were crowds of men, women and children. Some were cooking, others shouting, singing, dancing. They were the dirtiest people in Paris. They looked poor, and the houses of the square were old, ugly and falling down—but really the people were quite rich. They pretended to be poor and sick like the beggars who had run after Gringoire. They pretended to be poor and sick or blind so as to beg more money from the trusting, generous men and women. But now they were in their own square—the Beggar's Square, and the thieves, liars and murderers did not pretend to be without arms, legs or eyes. Many legless men were dancing, and blind men were playing cards.

"I can't believe it," thought Gringoire; "this can't be real! I must be asleep in bed, and this is all a terrible dream. I can't believe my eyes!"

But it was not a dream, The three beggars were shouting round him:

"Take him to the King! Take him to the King!"

Other beggars came and made a ring round him, and they all joined in the shout:

"To the King! To the King!"

"Their King must be the Devil!" thought Gringoire as the beggars fought to get near to him. But the three beggars shouted at the others:

"He's ours! Leave him to us! He's ours!"

They seized him, scratched him with their long, broken nails, and shouted:

"To the King! He's ours!" and, while they shouted, they pulled him along.

"O My Lady, Mother of Jesus, help me!" he prayed. "Have mercy on me and save me from these devils!"

Four

THE BROKEN CUP

Gringoire saw that he was in a kitchen, but it looked as if it belonged to the Devil. Men and women with hot dirty faces were sitting there, drinking wine. The lamps dropped oil onto broken tables. Some of the men were pulling cloths off their arms and legs and rubbing off "wounds"—not real wounds, but wounds painted on their skins. Others were cleaning black paint from their eyes so that they did not look blind. Laughter and dirty songs filled the air. A child, stolen from its wealthy mother, was sitting on a table and hitting a tin pot with a spoon.

"Come along!" shouted the first beggar, and he pushed Gringoire towards the fire. Near it sat a big man with a gold crown on his head. He looked like a gipsy. A great black dog lay at his feet.

"Take your hat off in front of our King!" cried the second beggar. Gringoire felt his old hat seized from his head. He looked around, but his hat had already disappeared. He nearly fell over a child rolling on the floor in the dirt.

"Stand up, you fool!" shouted an angry voice.

"Who is this fellow?" asked the King. He pushed a sharp stick at Gringoire: "Who is he?"

"Master . . . my lord . . . King . . . what must I call you?" Gringoire asked.

"Call me anything you like. But hurry up and defend yourself."

"Defend myself?" whispered Gringoire. "Defend myself against what?"

"Don't waste my time," cried the King. "I'm your judge. You have come into my Kingdom of Beggars. No one asked you to come. You must pay for coming. Now, who are you?"

"Please, lord . . . I am a writer. . . ."

"That's enough!" shouted the King. "Writers always speak evil of my people, the beggars."

"But I am Gringoire the poet, and my plays . . ."

"I saw one of your plays. It was bad, very bad. The man who wrote it should certainly be hanged."

"But surely you will not kill me without hearing what I have to say?" cried Gringoire.

A child threw a jar of oil into the fire, and it

burned more fiercely than ever. There were shouts and laughter. Some meat which was being cooked burned with a strong smell and a cloud of smoke.

"Mind my supper, you fool!" called a thick voice.

"Silence!" shouted the King of the Beggars. He made a rude sign to some men at the end of the kitchen, and then turned to Gringoire: "I don't see why you shouldn't be hanged."

Gringoire was white with fear.

"But," the King continued, "you good men don't seem to like being hanged, do you? And, after all, we don't want to do you any harm. Now let me think . . ." and the King rubbed his hand up and down his dark face.

"I know," he said at last. "There is a way out: you can become one of my men, a thief like the rest of us. What do you say?"

Gringoire breathed again at this chance of saving his life.

"O yes, I will!" he cried, "I certainly will!"

"Do you agree to march under my flag?"

"Yes, yes, I'll march under it wherever you tell me to go!"

"A thief among thieves?"

"A thief among thieves!"

"On your soul?"

"On my soul!"

"I must tell you that you'll be hanged for that, of course."

"Shall I?" whispered Gringoire, who felt hot and cold with fear.

"Only you'll be hanged by the honest men of

Paris on a fine gibbet in a more splendid way: so that's some comfort, isn't it?"

"Yes, it is, it is!" answered Gringoire.

"And you won't have to pay any money to the government: the whole city of Paris will be free to you!"

"Yes, yes it will!"

"And you're willing to be one of my men?"

"Certainly."

"It isn't enough to be willing. Good will is no use, except for going to heaven. If you want to be one of my people you must prove that you're good at our trade. Come, you shall steal from George, our little man."

"I'll steal from anyone you like," said Gringoire.

The King made a sign, and several men left the circle to get something. They came back a moment later with two wooden posts and stood them up on the floor. They fixed a third piece of wood across the top, and from that they hung a piece of rope. All this made a perfect gibbet.

Gringoire felt very troubled. "What will be the end of all this?" he said to himself.

The noise of little bells stopped him thinking. It came from the figure of a man, made out of cloth, which the thieves were hanging from the rope on the gibbet. The figure was clothed in red, completely covered with little brass bells. They rang prettily for a time as the rope swung, but their music became quieter and quieter and faded into silence when the figure became completely still.

The King pushed his stick towards an old chair which stood under the red figure, and said to Gringoire:

"Get up on that."

"The devil!" said Gingoire; "I shall break my neck! One leg of the chair is much shorter than the other three."

"Get up," repeated the King, quietly.

Gringoire stood up on the chair, waved backwards and forwards a few times, but he did not fall off.

"Now," said the King, "make yourself as tall as you can."

"Do you want me to break some of my bones?" asked Gringoire.

The King shook his head. "Listen, friend," he said, "you talk too much. This is what you must do: make yourself as tall as you can, so that you'll be able to reach the red pocket of our little George. Push your hand in, and pull out the money hidden in it. If you do all this without the sound of a bell, well and good—you shall be one of my people."

"I'll take great care," said Gringoire. "But if the bells on George do ring . . . ?"

"If the bells ring, you shall hang in his place, my friend. Now get to work, and no more talking. And remember, if a single bell makes the faintest little bit of music, up you go, by the neck!"

All the thieves made a circle round the gibbet; they shouted and laughed without any pity in their voices. Gringoire saw that he had no hope unless he did as he was told. He looked up at George, and

B

prayed eagerly to the red figure: its heart was sure to be softer than the hearts of the thieves who stood and watched. The brass bells looked like angry bees waiting to attack him.

Gringoire thought of one last hope, turned to the King and asked:

"And if there comes a breath of wind, to make the bells ring?"

"You shall be hanged," the King replied at once.

Finding that there was no way out, Gringoire set about his task. He stood as high as he could, and slowly stretched out his arm. But the moment that his fingers touched the red cloth he felt himself falling off the chair, and to stop himself he caught hold of George. At once all the bells began to ring, and, with their music sounding angrily in his ears, Gringoire fell to the floor. George swung backwards and forwards above him between the two posts.

"Help!" shouted Gringoire, as he fell; and he lay with his face to the floor as if he were dead.

The bells went on ringing, and the thieves laughed.

"Lift the fellow up, and hang him immediately," said the King.

Gringoire got up by himself. The thieves had already taken George down to make room for Gringoire. They lifted the poet onto the chair, and the King put the rope round his neck.

"Goodbye, friend," said the King. "You won't escape now: not a chance!"

The word 'mercy' died on Gringoire's lips: he

looked round, but saw no glimmer of hope; the faces all laughed like devils.

"Now you three," said the King; "one go on the top bar, one stand to knock the chair away, and one to pull his feet."

The three beggars who had brought in Gringoire now came to him. The little one with the black beard climbed quickly onto the bar and laughed down into Gringoire's face. The other two stood below, and waited to do as they had been told.

"When my stick hits the table . . ." said the King. With his foot he slowly pushed some bits of wood into the fire. There was a breathless silence.

"Are you ready?" he asked.

"Ready!" said the three in dry voices.

"Are you ready?" he asked again, lifting his stick in the air. His arm was still, waiting: a second more, and . . .

But he stopped, as if struck by a sudden idea.

"Wait a moment," he said. "I had forgotten our custom not to hang a man before we ask if there's any woman who will have him. It's your last chance, friend: you must either marry one of our women, or marry our rope."

Gringoire breathed once more.

"Now," said the King, "come along, you women and girls! A man for nothing! Who will have him?"

The women did not like the look of him.

"Hang him! That will amuse us!" one of them cried. Many laughed.

Three others, however, came out of the crowd to look at him. The first, a large young woman with a square face, looked closely at his poor clothes.

" Let me see your coat," she asked him.

" I have lost it," said Gringoire.

" Your hat? "

" They have taken it from me."

" Your shoes? "

" There's not much left of them."

" What's in your pocket? "

" Nothing, I'm sorry to say: not a penny! "

" Let them hang you; I don't care," she said, and turned away.

The second woman, old and dark, walked round him.

" He's too thin," she said, and left him.

The third was young, with quite a pretty face.

" Save me! " whispered the poor man. She looked at him with pity, then looked at the floor. She could not decide. He watched every move she made: it was his last hope. Then she made up her mind.

" No," she said; " Henri would beat me." And she went back to the crowd.

" Nobody wants the poet, then? " said the King. " Going . . . going . . ." and he turned his head to the gibbet as if to give the last word.

At that moment a cry went up from the other end of the room:

" Esmeralda! Esmeralda! "

Gringoire started, and turned. The crowd opened to make way for a clean, bright figure. It was the gipsy girl.

"Esmeralda!" whispered Gringoire in a voice full of wonder.

Her grace and beauty lit up the room, and the hard faces of the cruel thieves softened as she passed them. Her little goat, Djali, followed her.

She came to Gringoire, who was more dead than alive. She looked at him for a moment in silence.

"Are you going to hang this man?" she quietly asked the King.

"Yes, sister," he said; "unless you will take him as your husband."

"I will take him," she said.

Gringoire felt sure that he must have been dreaming ever since morning. They undid the rope and helped him to get down from the chair. Without a word the King took a cup from the table and gave it to Esmeralda. She put it into Gringoire's hands.

"Throw it to the ground," she said.

The cup broke into four pieces.

"Brother," said the King, laying his hands on their heads, "she is your wife. Sister, he is your husband—for four years. Go your ways."

Five

THE MARRIAGE NIGHT

The little room was very warm and comfortable: Gringoire sat at a table, and Esmeralda brought things from a shelf so that he could have his supper.

She paid no attention to him at all, as she passed

with a plate, a knife and a cup. He watched her, and felt as if he were in a fairy story. While she moved, Esmeralda spoke to her little goat: the words were too quiet for Gringoire to hear. At last she came and sat down near the table, and he could really look at her.

"How beautiful she is!" he thought. "And this lovely girl, who dances in the streets, has saved my life. She must love me madly, to have taken me as she has done. And now I am her husband!"

He got up, went to her, and smiled. But she drew back.

"What do you want?" she cried.

"How can you ask, my beautiful Esmeralda?" he replied.

"I do not know what you mean," she said.

"What! Am I not yours, sweet friend?—And are you not mine?" He put his arm round her.

Like a snake she escaped from his arm. She ran to the other end of the room and turned towards him with a little knife in her hands. Her eyes were bright with anger. At the same time the little white goat placed itself before her, and moved its head with its sharp golden *horns,* as if to tell Gringoire to keep away.

Gringoire looked at the goat and the gipsy.

"By Our Lady," he said, "what is this trick which you are playing on me now?"

There was silence.

"You must be a brave man," she said at last, "to come so near Esmeralda!"

"Forgive me, dear lady," said Gringoire with a smile; "but why did you marry me?"

"Was I to let them hang you?"

Djali moved his horns as if warning Gringoire to keep away

"So," said he, with his hopes of love sadly fading away, "you had no other aim in marrying me than to save me from the gibbet?"

"And what other aim do you think I could have had?"

Gringoire bit his lip. "Well," he said, "I am not such a successful lover as I had hoped to be! But then what was the use of breaking that cup, if you did not want me as a husband?"

Esmeralda's knife and Djali's horns were still pointing at him.

"I see," he said, "that I may not get any love: but I do need some food after all that has happened to me today."

Esmeralda did not speak. She threw up her head like a bird, and then laughed. The little knife disappeared as it had come, without Gringoire being able to discover where it was hidden.

A moment later a loaf of bread, a piece of meat, some wrinkled apples and a jug of wine were on the table. Gringoire began to eat eagerly. The loud noise of the knife on the plate showed that love had turned into hunger.

Esmeralda, seated near him, looked on in silence. She was busy with some thoughts of her own. She smiled from time to time, while her hand touched the head of the goat and pressed it softly against her knee. The lamp cast a yellow light on them.

When Gringoire's first hunger was satisfied he felt ashamed because only one apple and a bit of bread were left.

"Esmeralda," said he, "you are not eating."

She shook her head, but did not answer: she was lost in her thoughts. Gringoire wondered what they were. He spoke her name, but she was still silent. He spoke it once more, and once more she took no notice. But the goat did, and gently began to pull the girl's dress.

"What do you want, Djali?" asked the gipsy.

"Djali is hungry," said Gringoire, pleased to be able to start talking to the girl. Esmeralda took the bread and broke a little of it in her hand. Djali ate it.

Before she had time to start thinking again, Gringoire asked, in a sad voice: "Then you will not have me for your husband?"

She looked calmly at him, and answered: "No."

"For your lover?"

"No."

"For your friend?"

She thought, and then replied: "Perhaps."

"Do you know what friendship is?" he asked.

"Yes," she answered; "it is to be like brother and sister—two souls that meet, but do not mix—two fingers on the same hand."

"And love?" he went on.

"Oh, love!" she said, with her eyes shining brightly, "that is to be two and yet to be one; it is heaven!"

As she spoke she looked more beautiful than ever.

"What sort of a man will please you?" he asked.

"A soldier with a sword in his hand. He is armed

from head to foot, and he is riding a fine horse."

"And do you love such a man?"

"I shall know soon," she said.

"But could you not love a poet?" asked Gringoire in a quiet voice; "could you not love me?"

She looked at him seriously, and said: "I cannot love a man who cannot protect me."

Gringoire coloured as he remembered how little he helped her in the street two hours ago. The struggle came back to his mind, and he asked:

"How did you escape from the hands of Quasi-modo?"

"Oh, the nasty hunchback!" she cried. She hid her face in her hands, and shook as if with cold.

"Nasty indeed," said Gringoire. "But how did you get away from him?"

She smiled, and silently returned to her thoughts. Then she began to sing very quietly. Gringoire broke into the song to ask:

"Why do they call you Esmeralda?"

"I don't know," she replied. "Perhaps because of this." She drew from her dress a small bag which hung on a silver chain round her neck. The bag was covered in green silk, on which a piece of bright green glass was fixed.

"People say that there is a precious stone, bright green like this, and we gipsies call it 'La Esmeralda'."

"It is beautiful," he said, putting out his hand to the bag.

"No!" she cried, "do not touch it: it has magic power." She put it away again in her dress.

"Who gave it to you?" he asked; but she put her fingers to her lips and would not answer.

"Are your father and mother alive?" he asked.

She began to sing the old song:

"A bird was my mother;
My father, another;
Over the water I fly in the air,
Over the water without any care;
A bird was my mother;
My father, another."

"I came to Paris last year," she said. "When we walked under the gate, Djali and I, a little bird flew out, and I said, 'This will be a hard, cold winter.'"

"And it has been!" Gringoire cried. "I've done nothing but blow on my icy fingers. You are a prophet!"

"No," she said.

Then Gringoire spoke about himself.

"I have no father or mother," he told her. "They died when I was a baby. I was taught by the priests, so that when I grew up I could become a priest and a teacher in my turn. The priests were very learnéd. Even Claude Frollo, the most learnéd in Paris, gave me lessons once! But I wanted to be a writer, and that's what I am. No," he continued sadly, "that's what I was. But I couldn't get enough money to buy my bread. How shall we two live, now that we are man and wife?"

He waited for her to speak, but she was looking at the floor. Then she said, very quietly:

"Phoebus . . . Phoebus." She looked up at him.

"What does that word mean?" she asked.

Gringoire did not understand why she wanted to know, but he was pleased to be able to show his learning.

"It is a word in another language," he said, "and it means 'the sun'."

"The sun!" she repeated, with a beautiful smile, "the sun!"

"Phoebus was a god, noble and bright."

"A god!" she said, in a voice full of thought and wonder.

Then, before Gringoire understood what was happening, she ran out of the room. Her goat jumped quickly behind her. She shut the door. Gringoire stood up and hurried to follow her. Then he heard the key turn. He beat on the door till his hands hurt.

"So I shall have to spend my marriage night alone," he said sadly. "I hope that she has at least left me a bed!"

All he could find in the room was a long wooden chest, and he lay down on that. He was so tired that he went to sleep at once.

Six

THE PILLORY

The soldiers caught Quasimodo in the street, when he tried to carry away Esmeralda; they took him to prison. There he spent a night of fear. On the next morning he appeared in front of the judge in court.

Quasimodo could not hear a word that was said there. When questions were asked, he could see that he was being spoken to, and he watched how the lips moved. Then he replied as best he could. But his answers had nothing to do with the questions, and soon the court was full of laughter. The judge became very angry. He had been to a big, important dinner the night before: his stomach felt uncomfortable from too much food, and his head was very painful from too much wine. He thought that this hunchback with one eye was trying to make fun of him, especially as the judge's own ears were not very good either—though he pretended that he could hear everything perfectly, and people were afraid to point out his mistakes to him.

The judge had started late; and he had to listen to many cases that day; so he quickly finished with Quasimodo. He ordered the hunchback to be put on the Wheel and beaten for one hour.

Quasimodo could not hear a word that the judge had said, so he began to speak again:

"Perhaps you want to know my name now? It is Quasimodo . . ."

"Silence in court!" an officer shouted. But Quasimodo could not hear.

"I ring the bells in the church of Notre-Dame . . ."

"Silence in court! Silence in court!"

"And my age . . ."

The judge was so angry that his yellow face turned bright red.

"Take that man out!" he shouted, "and keep

him in the *pillory* for one extra hour. That will teach him a lesson! It doesn't pay to make fun of the Law, my man! "

And Quasimodo was seized and pulled away while the judge went on to the next case.

The Wheel was on the top of a stone tower beside the gibbet, in the Place de Grève. There was nothing inside it except some steep, rough steps which led to the top. On the top there was a big wheel: wrongdoers were tied to the wheel in a painful way, with their backs up and their arms close to their knees. Then they were beaten and, at the same time, the wheel was turned slowly round and round so that everybody in the square could see them suffer. Quasimodo was led to his pillory.

When he came into the square the night before, Quasimodo was carried with shouts and laughter and music as the High Priest of Fools. The crowds wanted him then. Now, they had no idea what wrong he had done, but their hearts were turned to stone as hard as the stone of the pillory, and they came to make him suffer more.

Sister Gudule looked out between the bars of the Rat-Hole as she heard people pass on their way to the Wheel in the Place de Grève. She pushed her head through, and her eyes shone with a mad light, as she cried to a soldier going along:

" For the love of God, let it be a gipsy! Let it be a gipsy who is beaten today! "

" Your prayer won't be answered this time, Sister," he said, with a laugh as he hurried along.

"My curses on them!" she shouted, "I curse all the gipsies!" She drew her head back into the Rat-Hole, lay down on the cold, dirty floor, and said her prayers.

The soldier joined the crowd round the pillory, and watched what was happening to Quasimodo. The hunchback's arms were tied so firmly that the ropes cut through the skin. He did not seem to feel any pain, or to understand at all what the people were doing to him. He took so little notice that he might have been blind.

The men pushed him onto his knees on the Wheel: he did not try to help himself in any way. They took off his coat and his shirt, and tied him down with chains; but still he did not move. Only he breathed sometimes with a loud noise, like an animal before it is killed.

The crowd laughed when they saw Quasimodo's back without any clothes, and they thought his ugly shoulders covered with red hair looked very funny. To those people without pity he was like a creature in a show.

The torturer went up the steps in the tower and stood by the Wheel. The word *torture* means great pain, terrible pain. The Torturer was a man employed to give terrible pain to men who had done wrong, or by terrible pain to force prisoners to speak the truth. The crowd shouted with joy when they saw him appear.

He put a tall *hour-glass* beside the Wheel: it was like two cups: the top cup was full of red sand, which fell through a neck into the bottom one. The sand took one hour to run down. All that time, Quasimodo was to be beaten.

Next, the torturer got ready to beat Quasimodo with ropes tied to a black stick. The ropes had many knots in them, and there were sharp pieces of metal on the ends.

Everything was ready: the torturer made a sign, the Wheel began to go round, and there was an excited buzz from the crowd. Quasimodo's face was full of surprise as he felt himself moving. The torturer raised his arm, and the first blow fell on the shoulders of the poor hunchback.

Quasimodo made a movement as if he had just woken from sleep. His body shook with pain, but he gave no sound. Only he turned his head, first to the left and then to the right, like an animal who tries to get a fly off its back. The people shouted.

The ropes fell on his shoulders a second time—then a third—then again—and again. The Wheel turned round and round, and the ropes kept on hitting him. Soon, blood ran down Quasimodo's back and shoulders, while the white ropes became red. Then the hunchback fought to get free. His eye was bright with fear, and he gathered all his strength against the chains which held his body down.

It was no use: he could not break away. So he gave up, and seemed to take no notice. He did not move at all, although the torturer became more and more angry and tried as hard as he could to wound the hunchback. Quasimodo's eye closed.

At last the red sand had all run down into the bottom of the glass. The first terrible hour was ended. An officer of the court, who sat watching on a big black horse, pointed with his spear towards the red sand. The torturer stopped. The Wheel stopped. The hunchback's one eye slowly opened.

Two soldiers rubbed some healing oil into the wounds on Quasimodo's back, so that the blood did not run any more. Then they covered his back with a yellow cloth. The torturer washed the blood from the rope in a bucket of water.

But all was not yet over for the hunchback. He had to stay for one more hour on the pillory. So the glass with red sand in it was turned the other way up, and he was left tied to the Wheel.

The people in the crowd hated the hunchback because he was so ugly. They shouted at him: but he could not hear. They threw stones at him, and those did hurt him. He bore the pain for a time without moving; but then, as he looked down at the hard, laughing faces he hated them and began to struggle. That made the Wheel begin to turn and so the crowd laughed even more. He gave up, like a wild beast which cannot break the chain holding its neck. The feelings that boiled in his blood made his face look darker and darker.

A priest on a donkey rode through the crowd. Quasimodo saw him, and the dark cloud in the face of the hunchback began to pass away. The sight of Claude Frollo made him feel happy, and he smiled. But when Frollo came close enough to see who the man on the pillory was, he quickly looked at the ground and—before Quasimodo could speak to him or show that they knew each other—turned his donkey away and kicked the beast to make it hurry back through the crowd.

A cloud, darker than before, covered the hunchback's face again; and his smile became sad, and then faded away.

Time passed. He was there for nearly an hour and a half, and he did not speak one word. But now he struggled once again in his chains, so that the Wheel shook from side to side, and with a noise that was like a dog's howl he cried out at the top of his strange voice: "Water!"

The crowd laughed at his cry and made fun of his thirst. They would not help him. His tongue hung out, and his eye rolled.

The red sand ran down the glass for a few minutes, and then again, in a more terrible voice, came the cry: "Water!"

Everyone laughed.

"Drink this!" shouted a man: he picked up a bit of wet cloth from the dirty street.

"Use this to get rid of your thirst!" called another, and he threw a broken cup at the hunchback's head.

"Water!" cried Quasimodo for the third time.

Then, out of the crowd came a girl, with a little goat behind her—the girl whom he had tried to carry away the night before. Esmeralda ran up the steps of the pillory, with a bottle in her hand. Without a word she opened the bottle and raised it to the lips of the poor man. Tears came into his eye. She pressed the bottle to his mouth.

He drank deeply. His thirst was burning.

When he had drunk enough, he put out his black lips to kiss the hand which helped him. But Esmeralda, remembering his attack of the night before, drew back her hand, like a child who is afraid of being bitten by an animal.

Even the crowd was moved by the sight of this beautiful girl, standing over the broken man on the pillory. A moment before this their laughter had wounded him: now they felt pity and shouted out that the girl had done well.

At that moment Sister Gudule, from her Rat-Hole, caught sight of Esmeralda.

"My curses on you, you evil gipsy!" she cried, "my curses on you for ever!"

Seven

SPELLING THE SECRET

More than two months passed: the evening in early spring was warm and sweet, and Notre-Dame looked very lovely.

On the other side of the road, a fine house at the corner shone in the red light of the setting sun. Upstairs, near the window, sat a party of pretty girls in beautiful dresses. All the girls were from wealthy families, and they had come to visit their young friend, Fleur, who lived in the house with her mother—a fat, rather silly woman. Fleur's father was dead.

Fleur sat a little apart from the other girls. She was talking to the young man whom her mother expected her to marry—Captain Phoebus de Châteaupers. Fleur's mother smiled at them.

"What a lovely pair they make, don't they?" she said to Alice, a dark girl who was Fleur's best friend. But Captain Phoebus was secretly tired of his pretty Fleur already. He could not think of anything that he wanted to say to her; he stood silent, and rubbed the top of his sword, or played with a button on his coat.

Fleur looked up at him. "Didn't you tell us," she said, "that you saved a gipsy girl some months ago?"

"I think I did," he replied.

"Well," she continued, "perhaps that is the same girl who is now dancing below, in the open place in front of Notre-Dame. Come and see."

She led Phoebus to the large window built out over the street: then she put her hand on Phoebus's arm. "Look down there," she said. "Is that your gipsy dancing?"

Phoebus looked, and smiled:

"Yes—I know her by her goat."

"What a pretty goat!" cried Fleur. The other girls came to the window also.

"Can you see, Monique?" Alice asked her little sister, holding her up to get a better view.

"Pretty, pretty goat!" shouted little Monique.

"With golden horns growing out of her sweet head! How lovely!" cried Fleur, and she smiled up at her Captain Phoebus.

Fleur's mother had not moved from her chair:
" Is that one of those gipsies, dear?" she asked, "I
say they should not be allowed into Paris: they are
dangerous, dirty people. Never trust them."

"Look at that man up there!" cried little Monique, "—that man dressed in black."

"Where, dear?" asked Fleur. Monique pointed
to a figure on the north tower of Notre-Dame. He was
a man in black clothes: his head was on his hands and
he was looking down at gipsy dancing. He stood so
still, so motionless as if he were part of the tower.

" It is a priest," said Fleur.

" How he is looking at the little dancer!" cried
Alice. " He is like an evil black bird waiting to fly
down, pick her up and carry her away!"

"She does dance beautifully," said a girl in a blue
silk dress.

"Phoebus," cried Fleur suddenly, "as you know
this gipsy girl, wave to her to come up!—She will
amuse us. Do let her come, Mother: we won't let
her make us dirty, and if she tries to harm us—well,
our Captain will protect us, won't you, Phoebus?"

"Very well, dear," replied her mother; "so long
as brave Captain Phoebus is here!"

"Oh," said Phoebus, "I'm sure she has forgotten
me, and I don't even know her name. . . . But,
since you wish it, ladies, I will try." He put his
head out of the window, and called: "Little one
down below! Look here, little one!"

Esmeralda was not, at that moment, playing her
drum. She looked up, saw Phoebus, and suddenly
stopped dancing.

"Little one!" he repeated, and he waved his hand to her to come up.

She looked at him again; her face became as red as a rose, and she walked through the crowd towards the house.

In a moment, she appeared inside the door of the room, but she dared not move a step closer.

Until Esmeralda arrived, all the girls in the room tried to please fine Captain Phoebus. The girls were all nearly equal in beauty; but as soon as the gipsy appeared with her lovely face, the beauty of all the others seemed dim. They knew this and looked at her with freezing eyes.

Phoebus was the first to break the uncomfortable silence.

"What a pretty creature she is!" he said.

"Not bad," replied Fleur in a cold voice. "Rather pretty in her way."

The others whispered together.

"Dear girl," said Phoebus, stepping towards Esmeralda, "I don't know if you remember me?"

"Oh yes," she answered. "Yes, I do."

"She has a good memory," said Fleur.

"You escaped very quickly the other night," continued Phoebus. "Did I frighten you?"

"Oh no," said Esmeralda.

"What a lovely voice!" thought Phoebus: Fleur thought so too, and was beginning to feel unhappy. Need Phoebus talk to the girl so much and in such a friendly way?

"You left a very ugly fellow in your place," said Phoebus. "What did he want with you?"

"I don't know," said Esmeralda.

"Well, he paid for what he did, I can tell you! He was beaten and put on the Wheel."

"Yes! Poor man," said Esmeralda. She remembered Quasimodo on the Wheel. "Poor man! I was so sorry for him!"

The girls were whispering to each other again. "What a strange dress!" said Alice. "It's very ugly, isn't it?"

"Yes, it is," said another girl. "Look at her arms! So brown! I suppose they get burned by the sun."

"Her legs too," said another girl. "What a very ugly dress! I've never seen such an ugly dress!"

"Oh dear!" said the girl in blue silk. "I can see that the Captain takes fire easily at bright gipsy eyes!"

"And why not?" said Phoebus.

Fleur's mother suddenly gave a cry: "What's that? What's that thing? Get away, you dirty beast!"

It was the goat. It had arrived to seek its owner. As it hurried towards Esmeralda it caught its horns in the long dress of the lady in the chair. Esmeralda, without a word, got Djali's horns free. Then she knelt down with her head beside the goat's, as if to say that she was sorry for having left Djali behind.

Alice came close to Fleur and whispered: "Why didn't I think of it before! We've heard of her. This is the gipsy with the goat, who is said to do wonderful things by magic: she is a witch."

Fleur turned to Esmeralda: "Let your goat do

some of its tricks to amuse us: some of the tricks that it does by black magic! "

" I don't know what you mean," replied Esmeralda, with her hand on Djali's head.

At that moment, Fleur noticed a brown bag hanging round the goat's neck.

" What is that? " she asked.

Esmeralda looked at Fleur. " That is my secret," she answered quietly.

Fleur walked away; she very much wanted to know what the secret was!

" Come, gipsy," said Fleur's mother, " if neither you nor your goat can amuse us, what are you doing here? "

Esmeralda turned to the door without replying, and the girls watched her. Nobody saw little Monique, with a piece of cake in her hand, draw Djali into a corner and quickly untie the brown bag from the goat's neck to see what was inside. There were some small pieces of wood, each with a letter painted on it in red. Djali finished the cake while Monique emptied the bag onto the floor.

At the door, the gipsy turned. She stood still, looking at Phoebus with her eyes full of tears.

" By my soul! " cried Phoebus, " you shall not go like this. Come back and dance for us! And, by the way, what is your name? "

" Esmeralda," she said.

" Es-mer-al-da! What a name! " The girls laughed at a gipsy having such a grand name.

" Look, Alice, what a clever goat! " shouted little

Monique. "It can make a word! Is it a real word? What do the letters spell?"

Djali, with her golden foot, was pushing the letters in the way which Esmeralda had taught her. The girls ran to look at the word.

"Why it's P-H-O-E-B-U-S, Phoebus!" cried Alice. "'Phoebus'!"

Sure enough, that was the word spelt by the goat.

"And 'Phoebus' is the Captain's name!" Alice continued.

"So that," thought Fleur, "is her secret!"

She burst into tears and hid her face in her hands. "She is a witch!" Then she fell fainting to the floor.

"My child! My child!" called her mother. Then she turned and shouted: "Go, you evil gipsy, go this minute!"

Esmeralda gathered the letters into their bag, made a sign to Djali and ran from the room, just as Fleur was carried out of the other door.

Phoebus stood between the doors for a moment: he could not decide which way to go. Then, with a smile, he followed the gipsy.

Eight

FROLLO ASKS QUESTIONS

The man in black whom Monique saw on the tower was Claude Frollo. He had a little room in the tower of Notre-Dame, to which he went every evening to study. But the dancing of Esmeralda pleased him more than his books did—although he loved them very deeply. While the sun set, he stood and fed his eyes on her beauty in the street below him. Then he saw someone else.

From time to time a man in a red and yellow coat went round the crowd of people who were watching the dancer: then the man sat on a chair, close to Esmeralda, with the goat beside him.

"Who is the man?" the priest asked himself in an angry voice. "He can come very near to her, too near! When I have seen her before, she has always been alone with her goat." Frollo ran down the stairs, breathing heavily.

He passed a little window on the way down. Quasimodo was standing there, watching the street below. After his return from the pillory, Quasimodo did not ring his bells as often as before. It was pleasure, not weakness, which made him leave his bells. Their music reminded him of the beautiful gipsy who had been so kind to him. He stood among the bells with his heart full of joy, thinking of her, and he forgot to go on ringing.

Frollo did not see Quasimodo standing there. He hurried down. When he reached the street, he joined the crowd. But the gipsy had gone!

"Where is she?" he asked.

"She's just gone into that house over there," said the man beside him, "to give them a special dance or two, I suppose. That big house at the corner."

On the rich Persian cloth where Esmeralda used to dance the man in red and yellow was now trying to amuse the people. He walked round in a circle with his head thrown back, his face hot and red, and a chair between his teeth: a cat was tied to the chair. The man passed close to Frollo.

"I know who he is!" Frollo said to himself. "I taught him when he was studying to become a priest. Look at him now, a fellow who is trying to win money from the crowd with these foolish tricks!" Frollo called, when the man came round again:

"Pierre Gringoire, is this how you use the learning which I gave you? Shame on you."

Gringoire was so surprised that he dropped the chair and the cat into the crowd. The cat got free from the chair, and scratched the faces of an old man and two women! To escape from the anger of the people, Gringoire rushed into Notre-Dame. The priest followed him.

"Come up to my little room," said Frollo. They climbed the stairs.

"Now, Pierre," said Frollo, as they sat down among the books of the learned priest, "tell me how you came to be playing the fool like that."

"It is poor work, I know," said Gringoire, "not so grand as a writer's. But it brings me some money and a man must live somehow, especially if he's married."

"Married!" cried Frollo. "Married? And who has the pleasure of being your wife?"

"You may not think much of her," said Gringoire; "she's only a gipsy. . . ."

"A gipsy!" shouted the priest, with a terrible look in his eyes; "have you fallen so far from God that you make love to a gipsy?"

"But I never have made love to her," said

Gringoire. "On my soul, I have not, although she is my wife."

"This is very strange," said the priest. "When people are married . . ."

"Yes, indeed we are married, and I will tell you how we came to be man and wife."

So the poet told his story of his meeting with the gipsy King of the Beggars. He spoke about George, the red figure with the little bells, and about the broken cup.

"And so," he ended, "I am married to her; but we must not make love: she says we must not."

"I am glad about that!" said the priest.

"There is magic in the reason."

"Magic?"

"Yes, the Gipsy King told me," said Gringoire. "Esmeralda, as a little baby, was found by the gipsies, and she does not know who her father and mother are. But she believes that she will find them again one day, with the help of a little bag which she always wears round her neck. There is magic in the bag, but the magic will go as soon as she makes love to any man, even her husband."

"I see," said Frollo, who now looked happier. "And has no man tried to make love to her?"

"Not if he values his life!"

"Why? Who would kill him?"

"She would kill him herself with the little knife which she always carries hidden in her clothes. She has no fear," said her husband.

"No fear?"

"None," said Gringoire. Then he thought for a moment, and he added: "Yes, she is afraid of two people—of Sister Gudule, who shouts terrible words from the Rat-Hole, and of a man who wears the black clothes of a priest, and whose eyes shine like fire. Those eyes burned into her memory on the night when the hunchback tried to carry her away, and she thinks that they now follow her wherever she goes."

"A silly fancy!" cried Frollo, and he got up suddenly and turned to the window. "What a foolish girl she must be!"

"I tell her that it's all a bad dream, and I beg her to forget it," said Gringoire.

"You are right!" cried the priest. "Yes, I know you are right, Pierre. There is nothing for her to be afraid of."

"I try to comfort her. She is a sweet girl."

"Indeed?"

"I love her deeply. She is very kind, not only to me but to all creatures. She is wonderful in the care she takes of Djali."

"And who is Djali?" askd Frollo.

"Her goat with the golden feet and golden horns. I will tell you about the way Esmeralda teaches Djali." Gringoire explained how the gipsy made the goat practise the trick of tapping the drum to show the hour of the day, and the day of the month. Djali knew exactly how many times to hit the drum because of the way the drum was held.

"And," Gringoire said proudly, "Esmeralda only took two months to teach Djali how to spell 'Phoebus'!"

"'Phoebus'!" said Frollo. "Why 'Phoebus'?"

"I don't know," replied Gringoire. "Perhaps she thinks that it's a word with magic power. She often repeats it quietly to herself when she thinks that she's alone."

"Are you sure," Frollo asked, with a sharp look, "that it's not a name?"

"Name of whom?" the poet asked.

"How should I know?" said the priest.

"The gipsies seem to think that the sun is their god," said Gringoire, "but Esmeralda did not know, until I told her, that other people call him 'Phoebus'. She does seem to love the name. Djali can spell it right every time!"

The priest looked very thoughtful; then, suddenly, he turned to Gringoire and said to him in a low voice:

"Will you give me your solemn word that you have never made love to the gispy, and your promise that you never will?"

"I could give you my word and my promise if I wished," said Gringoire angrily. "But let me ask you a question now, in my turn."

"Speak, Pierre. I will try to answer."

"Is it any business of yours?"

The pale face of the priest was hot with anger. He was silent for a moment. Then he spoke:

"Listen, Pierre. If you make love to a gipsy, I tell you that your soul will burn in the Devil's fire for ever. Many books on the shelves in this very room will tell you that! Do not touch her."

"She is very beautiful," said Gringoire, sadly, "I am proud to be her husband."

"Now go!" cried the priest, with a terrible look, "go to the Devil!" and he seized the surprised Gringoire by the shoulders and pushed him out of the room.

Nine

THE CAPTAIN AND THE GIRLS

Frollo, alone in his room, fell on his knees and lifted up his hands in prayer. He closed his eyes tight and tried to think of God. Prayers came to his lips, but his mind was not filled with thoughts of God: it was filled with thoughts of the beautiful gipsy. Ever since he first saw her Esmeralda was in his mind all day, and she danced through his dreams all night.

Frollo said his prayers aloud. Then the bells began to ring, and he raised his voice, as if God could not hear his words above the music of the bells. The words became louder and louder, until the priest was shouting. But he did not think of a word that he spoke, and he did not think for even a moment about God.

"It is the gipsy!" cried Frollo. He rose from his knees. "I seem to see her in the arms of other men, and I cannot bear the thought of anyone having her when I cannot have her myself!" He walked up and down the room between his books, like a wild animal in a cage.

"I cannot bear it!" he cried. "I cannot stay here.

If I stay here I shall go mad. I must find her, wherever she is. Where shall I begin to search for her tonight?"

He stood still, and thought for a time.

"I know!" he said to himself, "I'll start at the big house at the corner over there. That's where she went to dance before I met her husband—the devil take him!" He picked up a little knife, hid it in his clothes, and went out of the room.

The bells rang loud, as if they were laughing at him, while Frollo hurried through the church and out into the night. Stars shone clear, like jewels, and the moon rose up in the sky.

The door of the house at the corner stood open. He hid in the shadows while some girls in fine clothes came out. He listened to them:

"I'm sure she'll feel better tomorrow," said one.

"Yes, indeed! Poor Fleur, I do pity her with all my heart," said another.

"Her mother was right about gipsies, wasn't she? Of course Phoebus shouldn't have asked her up!" cried a third. "But then he followed her out! That was worse than anything!"

"'Phoebus'?" said Frollo. "Phoebus! Then Phoebus is a man, as I feared, and I shall find him with the gipsy!"

The girls went along the street, and Frollo could hear no more of what they were saying. He ran to the house: the servant—a large, plain woman—was just about to close the door. When she saw him, she stopped.

"You've come to see my poor young lady," she said. "Kind priests, like you, don't waste time when they hear of people in trouble! Do come in, although the dear sweet girl is too ill to see any visitors—even a priest—tonight."

"I'll just come in for a moment," he replied, "so that you can tell me what really happened, and how Fleur is: then I'll come again to-morrow."

They came into the hall, and the servant told her story to Frollo. There were tears in her eyes when she spoke of Fleur, but she spoke of Captain Phoebus with hot anger.

"I always said that he was an evil man," she cried, "—not good enough to come within a mile of our beautiful Fleur!"

"Indeed," said Frollo; "and what do you know about him?"

"More than enough!" she said. "Listen to this!" and she drew the priest into a corner. "He goes after a different woman every week! His fine looks catch them, the fools! They love his strong shoulders and his beard and his brave walk: he can do anything he likes with those girls. And he does, too! I can even tell you where!"

"Can you?" said the priest, and he tried not to appear too eager.

"At the house of that old woman on the bridge of Saint Michel: the woman called Falourdel. And to think that our pure, beautiful Fleur . . . !"

Suddenly a bell rang from a room upstairs.

C

"I must go at once!" cried the servant. "She wants me now, our dear little girl does!" and she ran up the stairs without another word.

Frollo opened the door and stepped out into the street. His mind was burning with the fires of hell, and his hand was hot on the hidden knife as he went through narrow streets towards the bridge of Saint Michel.

Ten

AT THE HOUSE BY THE RIVER

One house on the bridge of Saint Michel looked older, smaller and dirtier than any of the others. The walls were rough outside, and if someone wanted to climb them he could easily do so. Yet the only reason for wanting to climb up such an evil house must be an evil reason.

The old woman called Falourdel looked like her house. She was bent double, and she shook as she slowly walked across to see who was knocking at the door. In her shaking hand she held a lamp: it swung from side to side and cast shadows which moved like giants on the dark grey walls.

"Who's there?" she cried, in her thin voice like an insect.

"Captain Phoebus," said a man outside, and she opened the door.

"Oh, it's you again," she said, as she lifted her

wrinkled face with its white hairs on her chin, "come in."

Captain Phoebus entered, followed by Esmeralda and the goat.

"The best room," Phoebus said sharply.

Esmeralda seemed frightened, but he took her by the hand and she looked happier. He gave a silver coin to the old woman, who put it in a box which stood on the dusty table.

They left the room, and a little boy came out of the shadows, silently picked out the coin and put it into his pocket. A stick, with dry leaves still on it, lay by the cold remains of a fire. The boy broke off a bit of wood and dropped it, with a dry leaf, into the box where the coin was before. He heard the people going upstairs: he knew that no one had seen him, and the box would not sound empty.

"I am a very clever thief!" he thought.

The room into which Phoebus led Esmeralda was small and dirty, and there was not very much furniture in it. The window of the room, which looked out over the river, was broken. The moon shone bright on the water and then clouds came. Esmeralda and Phoebus sat side by side.

"Oh, Phoebus," she said, "I feel that I am doing wrong!"

"In what way, my dear girl?" he asked.

"In coming here with you," she said.

"I had to work very hard and talk for hours to make you come," he said.

"I don't wish to break my old promise about

taking a lover," she said. "If I do, the magic will lose its strength and I shall never find my father and mother. But why should I need them now? " she asked happily, looking at him with tears of joy in her eyes.

"The devil take me, if I can understand you!" cried Phoebus.

She was silent for a moment; a tear fell, and then she spoke:

"Oh, I love you! " she said; "how I love you! "

"You love me!" he breathed, and he threw his arm round her.

Something darker than clouds covered the face of the moon at the window behind them: it was a man's head—but neither Esmeralda nor Phoebus saw him. Their eyes, like their thoughts, were all for each other. The priest, at the window, watched them: his eyes burned, and his lips were dry as he drew them back from his teeth.

"Phoebus," said Esmeralda, as she gently pushed Phoebus's arm away, "you are good—you are generous—you have saved me—me, a poor gipsy without mother or father. I have long dreamed of a fine soldier who would save my life. I dreamed of you, my Phoebus, before I ever saw you."

The captain looked very pleased with himself, as she continued: "The soldier of my dreams has beautiful clothes like yours, a grand air, a sword. Your name is Phoebus: it is a beautiful name. I love your name; I love your sword. Draw your sword, Phoebus, so that I can see it."

Something darker than clouds covered the moon

"Foolish child!" said the captain: he smiled, and drew his sword.

The gipsy looked at it, then she kissed it and whispered:

"You are the sword of a brave man: I love my captain!"

At the window, the priest—hot with anger—touched the point of the knife hidden in his own black clothes: it was sharp, and he smiled to himself.

"Listen, my dear . . ." said Phoebus, moving closer to Esmeralda. She moved away: "No, no, I will not listen. Do you love me? I want you to tell me if you love me."

"Do I love you, heart of my life?" cried the captain. He knelt beside her. "My body, my blood, my soul—all are yours. I love you, and I have never loved any but you!"

He had said this so many times to other girls, on so many occasions like the present one, that he now spoke his words like a splendid actor. The gipsy looked up with joy.

"Oh," she cried, "this is the moment when we should die!"

"Die! No, no, my sweet one." Then, with a laugh, he added: "I know a little lady in fine clothes who is burning with anger at this moment!"

"Who?" asked Esmeralda, suddenly anxious.

"What does that matter to us?" said Phoebus. "Do you love me?"

"Oh, how can you ask?" she cried.

"I know you do," he said; "and we shall be

wonderfully happy. We'll get a little room in a pretty street, and I'll make my soldiers march up and down under your windows. Then I'll take you to see the lions in the king's courtyard; they are beautiful wild beasts, and all the women love to see them."

For some minutes Esmeralda was carried away by the sound of his voice; she did not listen to his words.

"Yes, how happy you will be!" the captain continued, and his eyes shone.

She turned to him: "Phoebus—Phoebus," she said, in a voice full of love, "teach me about your God and your Church."

"My God and my Church!" he cried, with a loud laugh. "What the devil do you want with such things?"

"So that we can be married," she replied.

His face changed: "Why should people marry?" he asked in a harsh voice.

Esmeralda turned away: "But surely . . ." she whispered.

"My sweet love," he said, gently, "what are all these foolish ideas? Marriage is very fine, no doubt, but those of us who are truly in love don't need it."

The priest heard every word and saw every movement in the room.

Suddenly, Phoebus saw for the first time the green bag which she wore about her neck.

"What's that?" he cried, and he moved towards

her: he pretended to look at it, but he was much more interested in her than in the bag.

"Don't touch it!" she replied quickly. "It protects me. It will help me to find my mother and father again. Oh, leave me, Captain Phoebus! My mother! My poor mother! Where are you? Come and save me! Captain, have pity on me!"

Phoebus drew back, and said coldly:

"I see plainly, young lady, that you don't love me."

"Not love you!" cried the unhappy girl, and she put her arms round him, and drew him to a seat by her side. "Not love you, my Phoebus? Why do you speak as if you were my enemy, to break my heart? Oh come!—I am yours."

She wept as she continued to speak: "The magic power of my little green bag means nothing to me now: I have you, so I don't need a father or a mother. Let us not marry, since you don't wish to. I'll be your servant. Only love me, Phoebus! Gipsy girls need nothing except love. Give me your love!"

She smiled through her tears. Her face was lit up with a look of joy, as if she were in heaven, and she raised her eyes towards the window and the moon.

Suddenly, over the head of Phoebus, she saw a grey, tortured face—a face with the look of a lost soul. Beside this terrible face there was a hand which held a little knife. The face and hand were those of the priest: he had climbed through the window, and now he was there, in the room. Phoebus could not see him. The young girl was frozen with fear.

She could not move or even cry out. She saw the knife descend upon Phoebus and rise again red with blood.

She fainted.

As her eyes closed, she thought that she felt a touch upon her lips, a kiss as hot as fire: then, for her, everything was dark.

When she opened her eyes she saw soldiers were standing all round her. She saw men carry the captain away. He was covered in blood. The priest had disappeared, and the broken window which looked onto the river was wide open. She heard, as in a dream, a voice say:

"She tried to kill the captain!"

And another voice replied:

"Yes—by her black magic!"

Eleven

THE TRIAL

Esmeralda had disappeared. For a whole day Gringoire had not seen her. He went to the King of the Beggars.

"Esmeralda has disappeared. For a whole day she has not returned home."

"You are her husband," said the King of the Beggars: "you must try to find her."

" But how can I, all by myself? " asked Gringoire.

" I'll help you," said an old beggar; " I'll help you tomorrow."

"So will I! " said another.

" And I will too," cried a young man with a big, ugly nose, " I'll start tonight, this minute. We need Esmeralda here: she makes this inn bright and happy."

"Yes, we must find her! " shouted one of his friends. "Come on, fellows! " And he went out of the inn, followed by a great crowd of beggars.

But they did not find her that night, nor the next day, nor on the day after that. For a whole month they had no idea where Esmeralda was. She and Djali disappeared without trace.

One day, when Gringoire walked sadly towards the Court of Law, he saw many people standing outside one of its doors.

A young man came out; Gringoire stopped him:
" What's happening in there? " he asked.

" It is the trial of a girl for an attempt to murder a captain," he said. " They say she may have done black magic. So there are priests in court, crowds of them. It's an ugly business," he said; and he went on his way.

Gringoire went into the Court of Law. He followed a priest up the stairs into the great hall.

"Where's the prisoner? " Gringoire asked a tall man standing next to him.

"There," he said, " she is sitting behind that crowd. I can hardly see her myself, so I'm sure you can't see her at all. Her back is turned towards us. But you can see the old woman who is speaking now, can't you? Her name is Falourdel."

"Thanks," said Gringoire, and he began to listen to the old woman's ugly voice.

"And then," she said, "a goat came in: a real goat, with golden horns—just the sort of animal that a witch would have with her. I didn't like it at all, I can tell you! The goat followed the girl upstairs, and then the house was quiet for a time. I could hear them in my best room, the captain's voice and the girl's voice, but nothing else, until he suddenly gave a terrible cry and something heavy fell. I hurried up as quickly as I could: and there I found him, flat on the floor, with a knife stuck in the back of his neck!"

She stopped, and her listeners held their breath. After a moment she continued:

"There was blood all over the floor of my best room—blood everywhere. I haven't been able to wash the last of it off yet! Then the soldiers came. They carried away the poor captain, and the girl, and the goat too."

"And is that the end of your story?" asked a priest with a long, thin neck and black hair. He seemed to be an important person.

"No, Sir," she said; "the strangest thing is still to be told. On the next morning I wanted some money to buy two eggs: so I went to my box where I knew there was a silver coin. The coin had gone, and in its place I found a little bit of stick with a dry leaf on it!"

The old woman stopped, and a whisper of alarm went all round the crowd.

"A goat is often the friend of a witch," said the man beside Gringoire.

"And that dry leaf!" added a fat woman on the other side of him: "only black magic could turn a silver coin into a bit of wood and a dry leaf!"

The judge now spoke:

"Gentlemen," he said, "you have the papers which show all that Captain Phoebus has said."

At that name the girl who was being tried jumped to her feet: her head rose above the crowd. It was Esmeralda—but Esmeralda terribly changed!

Her face was white; her hair, beautifully kept before, now hung in disorder round her face; her lips were blue; her eyes looked terrible.

"Phoebus!" she cried; "where is he? Oh, Sirs! Before you kill me, have enough pity to tell me if he is still alive!"

"Be silent, woman," answered the judge; "that is no business of yours."

"Oh, mercy! Mercy! Tell me if he is alive," she repeated, holding up her beautiful, thin hands. Her chains made a cruel sound as they brushed along her dress.

"Well," said the judge in a rough voice, "he is nearly dead. Is that enough for you?"

The poor girl, unable to speak or to weep, fell back in her seat as if she were made of stone.

"Bring in the second prisoner!" shouted a man with a silver stick in his hand.

All eyes were turned to a little door, which now opened. Through it came a pretty goat with golden feet and golden horns. It stood still for a moment, and looked round: then it saw the gipsy, ran towards her, jumped over the table, and rolled at her feet as if to ask for a touch of her hand. But the poor girl did not move; she did not even look at Djali.

"That's her evil beast!" the old woman Falourdel cried; "I know the pair of them very well."

The priest with the long neck rose, and said in a high voice:

"If the black spirit in this goat frightens the court with its evil deeds, we must send the animal to the gibbet."

"To the gibbet!" whispered Gringoire. "What will they do to the poor creature there?" He saw the priest take Esmeralda's little drum from the table, and hold it out to the goat in a special way.

"What o'clock is it?" the priest asked the goat.

The goat looked at him with clever eyes, lifted a golden foot and hit the drum seven times. It was indeed seven o'clock. A movement of terror ran through the crowd.

Gringoire could not stop himself from crying out in his fear:

"The poor beast will kill itself: it doesn't know what it's doing!"

"Silence at the back of the hall!"

The priest moved the drum round, and made the goat show the day of the month. He moved it again, and the goat counted up to the month of the year.

A few weeks before, in the squares of the city, Djali's tricks filled the crowds with delight; now the same tricks produced only fear. The people were sure that the goat was a devil—a devil in the shape of a goat.

The priest took a brown bag from the goat's neck, and emptied pieces of wood from it onto the floor. Red letters were painted on the pieces, and with a golden foot the goat spelt the dangerous name: ' Phoebus '. The crowd cried out in terror and moved away from the goat.

Esmeralda gave no sign of life. She seemed to hear and see nothing. A big soldier shook her by the arm, while the priest cried to her:

" Do you still say that you did not, with the help of black magic and the evil powers of this goat, try to kill Captain Phoebus? "

" Oh, my Phoebus! " cried Esmeralda, and she hid her face in her hands. " My Phoebus! This is worse than death! "

" Do you say that you did not try to kill him? " the priest asked coldly.

" Kill him! " she cried in a terrible voice; " I would never wish to kill him—never! "

" Then how do you explain the things which we have heard and seen? "

She answered in a broken voice:

" I have already told you who tried to kill him. It was a priest—a priest whom I do not know—a priest who looks like a devil, and he follows me! "

" A priest like the devil! " he repeated, with a cruel laugh.

"Oh, gentlemen, have pity! I am only a poor girl . . ."

"A gipsy," said the judge.

The priest raised his hand and shouted:

"Because she will not speak the truth, I demand that she shall be tortured!"

"She shall be tortured," said the judge.

The poor girl shook with terror: but she rose, at the order of a soldier, and walked with firm steps down the hall. A door at the end of it opened, and then closed behind her. To Gringoire, it seemed like a terrible mouth which had just eaten her.

When she disappeared, a cry was heard. It came from the little goat.

Twelve

TORTURE

Esmeralda was led down many stairs and along many dark passages until she came to the room where prisoners were tortured. She stopped at the door.

"Go on!" said a rough voice behind her. "We don't want to waste time, do we? The sooner you tell us the truth, the sooner all this trouble will be finished. So come along quick!"

A soldier took her by the arm and pushed her into the room. It was dark, except for the red light from a big fire: there were no windows. Many pieces of iron, of different shapes, hung over the burning coal to become hotter and hotter: they were some of the instruments of torture. Others lay on the floor and more hung from the roof—strange, ugly shapes.

Esmeralda looked at these terrible things: "No, no!" she cried; "I can't bear it!"

"There's no need to bear any of these painful things," said a priest who followed her into the room. "You only need to say that you tried to kill Captain Phoebus by black magic, and then you can turn your back on these instruments and walk straight out of the door. See, we'll leave it open for you!"

Esmeralda lifted her frightened eyes and looked this way and that way, like a hunted animal. Dark men in rough clothes stood in the corners of the room, and the torturer himself sat, with his legs crossed, on a black, wooden bed. He looked at her; he stood up: his face was full of cruel hunger. She stepped away from him with a little cry.

The priest spoke again:

"Will you not tell us the truth?" he asked.

"I've told you already," she whispered, and she closed her eyes.

"Very well," he said in a harder voice; "we shall see what you say after the torturer has helped you to speak. Let's begin."

An officer in red clothes drew his sword, and with its point he touched a large shoe, made of wood, which lay under the bed.

"Start with this," he said. He smiled as he added: "It looks too big for our dancer's little foot; but you can make this shoe smaller, torturer, can't you?"

"We can make it fit any size of foot, big or little," he replied. "Yes, it's a fine old shoe, a real beauty!" He held it up in both hands and laughed.

Two soldiers took Esmeralda's arms and pulled her down onto the bed; the torturer fixed the wooden shoe round her right foot, and prepared to turn a piece of metal which would slowly bring the top and bottom of the shoe closer together and break her bones between. The girl's eyes were wide with fear.

"You're just in time," said the officer in red to someone who now came behind her into the room. It was the priest with a long neck: "Just in time with news to make her feel really happy!" he said, and he moved to Esmeralda and stood in front of her. The torturer remained still. After a moment, the priest spoke.

"Well, you succeeded, woman!" he said, as he looked down at her; "you succeeded: you killed him. Captain Phoebus died five minutes ago."

"Died!" she whispered; "Oh no! If he is dead, then I cannot live!"

"He is dead, and you killed him," said the priest. "You and your goat killed him with black magic, didn't you?"

There was a long silence. No one moved.

Suddenly the girl threw back her head. "Yes!" she cried, "yes!" Her eyes shone as she turned to the officer, "yes, I killed him! I killed him by black magic. That's what you want me to say, isn't it?"

The priest looked quickly at the officer; the torturer cursed quietly.

"We wanted the truth," the priest said; "and I know, my girl, that you have now, at last, given it to us. Thanks be to God!"

Her whole body shook, and she closed her eyes.

"Take off the shoe," the officer said to the torturer, who sadly did as he was told.

"My child," said the priest, and he took her cold
hand in his: "now that you have told the truth, you
have only to pay for Phoebus's death with your
death. You will be hanged very soon."

"I hope so," she said, in a voice empty of all
feeling.

The men helped her to her feet: she could hardly
stand. The officer had to carry her out of the door
and down the passage, to the room where she was to
stay until the day of her death on the gibbet.

Thirteen

A WAY OF ESCAPE

There were rooms deep in the ground in which
the most dangerous prisoners were kept alone to
wait for death. The rooms were small and far apart
from each other. No sound could be heard, and the
prisoners could not tell day from night because the
rooms had no windows. The walls and the floors were
wet, and cold as ice.

When Esmeralda heard of the death of Phoebus,
the sun went out of her life: she felt no wish to live.
Time stopped for her. The room was cold and dark
like a grave. When the thick door was opened she did
not notice it, at first. Then her eye felt pain, and she
saw that there was a lamp in the room: a man was
holding it. Slowly she began to think, and at last she
spoke.

"Who are you?" she asked.

"A priest."

She felt afraid, because the voice sounded in her memory: but she could not remember whose it was. Again the voice spoke:

"Are you ready?"

"Ready for . . . for what?"

"Ready to die," he said.

"Will it be soon?" she asked.

"Tomorrow."

"Why not today?" she whispered. "What difference would a day make to them?"

"Are you very sad?"

"I am very cold," she replied.

He looked down at her, where she sat on the wet floor. Her hands were thin and dirty, and she slowly rubbed her feet with them.

"Without light!" he said "Without fire! And all the room is wet: it is terrible!"

"Yes," she whispered. "The day belongs to everyone. Why do they give me only night?"

"Do you know why you are here?"

"I think I knew once," she said, and she closed her eyes and thought; "but now I do not know. I don't remember."

She began to weep like a child.

"I want to go away from here," she said. "I am cold and I am frightened."

"Then, follow me."

The priest touched her arm, and although she was cold his hand felt like ice on her skin.

"It is the hand of death!" she whispered; "who are you?"

Claude Frollo held the lamp close to his face and knelt beside her. She looked at him: then she pressed her hands to her eyes, and shook with fear.

"The priest!" she cried; "you are that priest!" and she tried to move away from him.

"Why do you look at me like that?" he asked. "Why are you so afraid?"

She did not answer.

"Why?" he asked again.

"It is the priest," she said in a low voice; "it is the priest who killed him—killed my Phoebus!" and she wept. Then, through her tears, she cried:

"What have I done to you? Why do you hate me? How have I ever hurt you?"

"I love you!" cried the priest.

Her tears suddenly stopped: she looked at him with empty eyes, as if she were mad.

"Do you hear? I love you!" he cried again.

"What love can you have for me?" she whispered.

"The love of a lost soul!"

For a long time they were silent; then, at last, in a strange, calm voice he said:

"Listen: I shall tell you everything, all the secrets that I have hidden even from myself . . . except in those dead hours of the night when it is so dark that God can hardly see us. Listen. Before I saw you I was happy. . . ."

"And I was happy too!" she cried.

"I must speak to you," said Frollo; "I must tell

you everything. I was happy; my soul was full of light. . . ."

He spoke, but she did not hear him. She was too weak to listen to the terrible story of his desire for her. On and on he spoke, as he knelt beside her on the cold, wet floor. She felt nothing: she saw nothing now except a wall of grey cloud pressed against her eyes. Then at last some of his words entered her mind.

"I killed him for you!" he cried, "for you! I can save you. Come with me now . . . I love you! We can live together in some little town far away. We can be happy!"

"I hate you," she whispered. "I have little strength left, but with all of it I hate you! I hate you now. Tomorrow I shall hate you, and tomorrow I die. Then I shall hate you for ever." She closed her eyes, and lay back against the wall.

With the cry of a wounded animal the priest stood up. She did not seem to hear him as he cursed her. He left her, and the door shut behind him, but still she did not move. Time passed. Then, slowly, she moved her weak hands and began to rub her feet.

"I am so cold—so cold!" she repeated again and again, and tears ran down her face.

Fourteen

THE ROPE

"Get out my way!" shouted Sister Gudule between the bars of her Rat-Hole. "I can't see through your thick head, young man!"

"All right, all right, old woman, there's nothing to look at yet." But the soldier stepped aside: "The cart hasn't come round the corner."

"Tell me when it does. I can't see much out of this window; I don't want to miss watching this gipsy go to the gibbet."

"You've got a hard heart, Sister Gudule, as hard as stone!" the soldier said.

"You know nothing about my heart or what it has suffered, so mind your own business!"

"You mind your manners, old woman," said the soldier, and he moved in front of the window so that she couldn't see. "Mind your manners, or I'll stay here all the afternoon!"

The people near him laughed.

"That's right!" shouted a fat man. "You teach her how to behave, soldier!"

"She's too old to learn," said his friend.

"Look!" cried a tall woman who stood beside them, and they all turned towards the corner: "here the witch comes!"

The people were silent as the cart came towards them. It was drawn by a big, grey horse, and soldiers in red and yellow rode beside it. They carried white crosses.

"I can't see," shouted Sister Gudule, "move out of my way!"

"Shut your mouth," said the soldier, but he stepped aside again. "One more word from you, and I'll come back, I promise you!"

Sister Gudule held the bars and pulled herself up

to see through them, but she was not high enough to catch sight of Esmeralda.

The poor girl sat as low as she could in the cart, to hide from the crowd. Her hands and feet were tied, and her head hung down in shame. She wore a white dress, and her black hair spread down on her shoulders. The man at the gibbet would soon cut it off, but now it blew in the wind: as it moved from side to side it uncovered the silver chain and the green silk bag which still hung round her neck. The pale, winter sun came out for a moment and the green glass on the bag shone brightly.

The horses made a noise—Clop! Clop! Clop!— as they came across the square, and the wheels of the cart rang on the stones: but the people made no sound. They were full of pity for the girl who sat, like a tired, lost child in the bottom of the cart. Her face was as white as her dress, and she seemed to be half asleep.

"She doesn't look as if she could murder a mouse!" said the soldier. "I don't believe she killed Captain Phoebus."

"Of course she did," said the tall woman, "by black magic."

"A witch need not have a strong body," said the fat man.

"Her power comes from her evil soul," the woman replied; "but she does look a weak creature."

"Where is she?" shouted Sister Gudule. "Is she in the cart? Is she there?"

"She's there, poor little girl," said the soldier.

"Listen, you gipsy," the old woman shouted from her Rat-Hole; "listen to the curses of a mother whose baby was stolen by your terrible people!"

The soldier turned angrily to Sister Gudule. He pushed his sword between the bars of the window until the point nearly touched her thin chest.

"Be silent!" he cried, "if you want to live."

Sister Gudule let go of the bars and knelt on the floor of her Rat-Hole, where the long sword could not touch her.

"Take my curses with you to the gibbet!" she shouted, "take my curses with you to your death!" Her voice rang out, cruel and hard, but Esmeralda did not seem to hear.

"Be silent!" shouted the people near the Rat-Hole, "the girl suffers enough."

The cry of an animal in pain came from the cart.

"It's her goat," said the tall woman. "It knows that it's going to be killed with her."

Djali lay at the feet of Esmeralda. Its legs were tied together, and it could only move its head: it did so now, turning from side to side, and it cried because the ropes cut into its legs.

"Poor Djali!" whispered Esmeralda; "but both our lives will soon end, and we shall be at peace."

The great doors of Notre-Dame stood open. Slow, sad music flowed out into the square where the crowd stood and waited beside the gibbet. A line of priests came through the doors: they were dressed in black; they walked slowly, and moved like a thick snake down the steps and between the lines of people.

Everybody's eyes were turned towards the cart; nobody thought of looking up, above the doors of Notre-Dame: a strange man was standing there, among the stone figures. He held a rope, and he tied one end of it to a stone *pillar*. The other end of the rope hung down to the square, against the grey, stone building.

When the rope was fixed as he wished it to be, the man stood still. He was Quasimodo, and he looked as ugly as the *gargoyles*—strange creatures cut in stone which pour rain-water from the roof of Notre-Dame through their mouths. Some birds flew past the hunchback, and he smiled as he waited and watched the square below him.

The cart stopped in front of the steps, and four men untied the ropes from Esmeralda and Djali. The goat gave a cry of joy when it could move its legs again, but Esmeralda looked with terrified eyes at the priests in front of her. Frollo was among them: his face was as white as death and his eyes as red as fire.

She saw him, and she nearly fainted: she nearly fell, but two men held her up and lifted her from the cart. The other men picked up the goat, and put it beside her. The singing from Notre-Dame came to an end, and Esmeralda and Djali stood and looked through the open doors into the great, dark church. The priests began to pray; their voices together sounded like a stormy sea.

Suddenly the hunchback took the rope in both his hands, held it between his knees and his feet, and

Quasimodo had tied a rope to a stone pillar

came down it as quickly as a monkey. He dropped onto the steps, ran between the priests, and stood in front of Esmeralda. In a moment, with his big, strong hands he knocked down the two men who held her; then he picked her up in one of his arms, picked up Djali in his other arm, and ran like a cat up the steps into Notre-Dame.

In a church, everybody is safe from the Law. No person had the right to touch the gipsy and her goat inside Notre-Dame: they were safe, as long as they stayed there.

"She is safe here!" Quasimodo turned just inside the doors, lifted Esmeralda above his head in one hand, and shouted, "She is safe!"

"She is safe! She is safe!" repeated the excited crowd.

The sound made Esmeralda open her eyes. She looked down at Quasimodo, then closed her eyes suddenly, because the hunchback who had saved her seemed too terrible to look at. His big, bushy head was like the head of a lion. He carried Esmeralda with as much care as if he feared to break her. He seemed to feel that a thing so beautiful was not made for his rough hands.

Then, all at once, he pressed her close to his ugly breast as if she were his own treasure, a precious child: he held her as her mother might have done. His eye rested on her, filled with grief and pity. Out in the square, the crowd saw that a beauty of his own shone through Quasimodo's terrible body. The women laughed and wept, and the men shouted. He was fine. He, that hunchback child without a mother or father, whom the people had thrown away, now felt that he was great and strong: he looked in the face of the people who had refused to let him live with them. He had beaten the power of their Law with the power of his God.

Quasimodo ran far into the church with Esmeralda in his arms. The goat ran after them, and its horns and its hoofs shone golden in the darkness of Notre-Dame.

The crowd stood still and wondered what would happen next. Then the hunchback appeared again: he was at the end of a passage high above the doors. He held the girl up in his arms, and shouted: "She is safe!" The crowd repeated his shout.

He disappeared, and then a moment later he showed himself higher up, carrying Esmeralda as if she were as light as a flower. Again the people shouted with joy, and again Quasimodo disappeared.

They saw him for the third time when he was on the top of the tower of the great bell: from there he seemed to show the girl to the whole city. His voice rang out three times in a shout of victory:

"Safe! Safe! Safe!"

The crowd shouted back with a great, happy cry which shook the bars of the Rat-Hole where Sister Gudule stood and cursed.

Fifteen

ABOVE THE CITY

Quasimodo brought Esmeralda to a little room under the roof of the tower. When she was in his arms she felt as if she were flying in her sleep. From time to time she heard his loud laugh and his rough voice: they seemed to come out of a dream. She half opened her eyes and saw, far below her, the roofs of Paris: then she looked up, and saw above her head the hunchback's ugly face made bright with joy. She closed her eyes and thought: " Perhaps I have died on the gibbet and my soul is being carried away by some strange creature—some spirit of the other world."

Quasimodo laid her down in the little room. She woke up: her eyes and her mind began to work again. She saw that she was in the tower; she remembered that she had been carried away from the men who were going to kill her; she turned to Quasimodo. "Why did you save me?" she asked.

He looked puzzled, as if he was trying to guess what she said. "Why did you save me?" He gave her a look of deep sorrow, and fled.

She was surprised; she did not understand that he was deaf.

A few moments later he returned with some clothes and laid them at her feet. A kind woman had left them for her at the doors of Notre-Dame. Esmeralda looked down at herself, and saw that she wearing only a thin, white dress. She turned away from Quasimodo.

Quasimodo seemed to understand. He put his broad hand over his eye and went slowly out of the room. Esmeralda put on the dress: it was very simple and warm.

She had hardly finished before Quasimodo returned: he carried a basket under one arm and bedding under the other. There was a bottle, a loaf of bread and some other food in the basket. He put the basket on the floor and said: "Eat." He spread out the bedding and said: "Sleep."

It was his own food, and his own bed, which the hunchback had brought her. Esmeralda lifted her eyes to his face to thank him, but she could not speak: the poor fellow was terribly ugly!

"I frighten you," he said. "I am very ugly, am I not? Do not look at me, only listen to me. In the day you will stay here; at night you can walk about anywhere in the church. But do not take a step out of it, either by night or by day. You would be lost: they would kill you; and then I would die."

She raised her head slowly to reply, but he was already gone. Alone once more, she thought about the strange words of the ugly creature, and about the strange sound of his voice, so rough but so gentle.

Then she began to look at her room: it was big enough for a bed, but that was all. There was a small window, and a low door which opened onto a roof of flat stones. Three of those stone animals pushed their heads out over her window so that the rain-water could flow through their long necks. The gargoyles were ugly, but much less ugly than the hunchback.

Beyond the roof Esmeralda saw many chimneys, from which rose the smoke of the fires of Paris. She thought of the families sitting round the fires in their homes, and she felt sad to be alone, unable to leave the room by day or the church by night. She sat on the bed and wondered what would happen to her.

Suddenly she felt a hairy head pushed between her hands. She looked down: it was Djali. She covered the goat's head with kisses. "Poor Djali," she said, "I had forgotten you, and yet you think of me!"

At the same moment, as if an unseen hand lifted the weight which for such a long time held back her tears, she began to weep: and, as her tears flowed, she felt the sharpest of her grief go with them.

When night came, she thought the darkness so beautiful; the moonlight was so soft. She walked all round the tower and looked down at the sleeping city. The earth appeared so calm when seen from high above. She could almost feel happy again, under the starry sky, with the city far down at her feet.

The next morning a bright beam of the rising sun shone through the window onto Esmeralda's face. With the sun, she saw at the window something which frightened her: it was the ugly face of Quasimodo. She closed her eyes again, in fear, but she heard a rough voice say very gently:

"Do not be afraid. I am your friend. I came to see

you sleep. You don't mind, do you, if I come and see you sleep? It does not matter to you if I am here when you have your eyes shut? I will go now. There! I am hidden behind the wall; now you may look again."

Esmeralda was touched by the sad sound of Quasimodo's voice. She opened her eyes: he had gone from the window. She went to it and saw the poor hunchback push himself against a corner of the wall. She tried to conquer the sick feeling which the sight of him raised in her.

"Come here," she said to him gently.

From the movement of her lips, Quasimodo thought that she told him to go away: he covered his eye, and moved back away from her.

"Come here, I say!" she called; but he continued to walk away.

Then she ran out of the room, hurried to him and took his arm. When he felt her touch him, his whole body shook. He looked at her with his one eye wild with grief: but, when he saw that she tried to draw him to her, his whole face shone with happiness. She tried to make him come into her room, but he would not.

He stood at the door, and she sat down on the bed and looked at him. Every moment she discovered a new beauty in his ugly body.

He was the first to break the silence. "So you really told me to return?"

"Yes," she said.

He understood what she meant from the movement of her head. Then he spoke, slowly and sadly:

"I am—I am deaf."

"Poor man!" said the girl, in a voice full of pity.

"Yes, I am deaf. That is the way I am made. I am very ugly. And you—you are beautiful."

He sounded so sad that she had not the courage to say a word. He continued:

"I never saw myself until now. I must look to you like a beast. You—you are like a beam of light from the sun, a flower, a bird. As for me—I am not a man, but I am not a beast."

Then he began to laugh, and his laugh was the saddest thing in the world. He went on:

"Yes, I am deaf, but you can speak to me by signs. I have a master who talks to me in that way. And then I shall very soon know your wish from the movement of your lips, and from the way you look."

"Tell me then," she said with a smile, "why you saved me."

He watched her carefully while she spoke.

"I understand," he answered. "You ask me why I saved you. You have forgotten a poor, bad man who tried to carry you away one night—a poor creature to whom you brought help the next day on their terrible pillory; a drop of water, and a little pity. That is more than I can pay back with my life. You have forgotten that poor creature, but he remembers."

This strange man filled her with sorrow. He began to move away. She made a sign to him to remain.

"No, no," he said, "I must not stay too long. It

D

is because you feel pity for me that you do not turn
away your eyes. I will go where I can see you without you seeing me; it will be better like that."

He took from his pocket a small, metal *whistle*.

"There," he said: "when you want me, when you
wish me to come, use this whistle. I can hear the
sound of this."

He laid the whistle on the floor and fled.

Sixteen

THE PLAN OF ATTACK

Time passed, and calm slowly returned to the
soul of Esmeralda. Too much sorrow, like too much
joy, cannot last long: our hearts cannot bear it.

The beauty of Notre-Dame helped to heal her
wounded thoughts. She listened to the solemn singing, and began to forget her pain. The grand music
made her want to live again, and when the people in
the church sang she wanted to sing too. Best of all,
she liked the music of the bells: their sounds flowed
over her mind and filled it with comfort.

She never blew the whistle which Quasimodo gave
her, but he came many times during the first few
days although she did not call for him. He brought
the basket of food and the bottle of water: but he
always noticed the slightest movement that she made
to turn from him, and then he went from the room
sadly.

One day he came at the moment when she was
playing with Djali. He stood for a time, watching

" When you want me, use this whistle. I can hear the sound of this."

the graceful picture of the girl and the animal. At last he shook his ugly, heavy head, and said:

" My hard fate is that I am too much like a man: I wish I were completely a beast, like that goat."

She looked at him with surprise.

To this look he answered, " Perhaps you cannot understand; but I—I know it too well! " and he went away.

Another time he came to the door of the room when Esmeralda was singing an old song from Spain: she did not know what the words meant, but they were still in her mind because the gipsy-woman had helped her to sleep with the song when she was a child. At the sight of Quasimodo's ugly face, which came suddenly in the middle of her song, she stopped singing with a movement of alarm.

Quasimodo held his big, ugly hands together, and cried:

"Go on, I pray you! Do not send me away."

She did not wish to cause him pain; she went on singing. Slowly her fear went from her, and she forgot him in the beauty of the song. He remained all the time with his hands joined together as if in prayer: he hardly breathed, and he looked into her beautiful eyes as though he could read the song there.

Another time he came to her and he seemed to be afraid.

"Listen," he said, although he had to struggle to speak the word. "I have something to say to you."

She made a sign to him that she was listening. Then he half opened his lips, looked for a moment to be about to speak, shook his head, and slowly went away from her, hiding his eye with his hands. Esmeralda was very puzzled.

Among the gargoyles outside her window, Quasimodo seemed to like especially one strange beast. Often he looked at it as if the beast could understand him. Once the gipsy heard him say to it:

"Why am I not made of stone, like you?"

The pity which Esmeralda felt for Quasimodo drove out of her mind the men who before had filled it with fear. She began to forget the torturer and the priest with the terrible eyes.

But the priest with the terrible eyes did not forget her. For many hours of every day he shut himself up in his room among his books and fought with his desire to go to her. There she was, in the next tower in the same building! But, although he often went to spy on her, he never dared to let her see him. He hid in corners and watched her when she walked in the church at night. He hid on the stairs and watched when Quasimodo visited her room during the day. All night and all day she filled his mind.

"See how the hunchback looks at her!" he said to himself one afternoon when he found them together. "I first saw that look on his face when he tried to carry her away and Captain Phoebus stopped him. And see how she looks at Quasimodo!"

Esmeralda's expression of sweet pity made Frollo very angry. He wanted to run between them, strike the hunchback and take her in his arms. But he

knew that he could not, and he rushed down the
stairs and into the church. The beautiful music
sounded like an evil noise to him, and he ran away
from it up the stairs to his own room as if he were
mad.

That night his dreams were more frightening than
before.

Another man who had ugly dreams about Esmeralda was the poet Gringoire. He was in the crowd
when Quasimodo ran with her and Djali into Notre-
Dame.

"Thank God!" cried Gringoire when he saw
that she was safe, and he shouted with joy until his
voice lost all its strength. Then he began to wonder
how he could find her again.

"I am her husband," he said to himself, "and I
must try to get her back. She can't live in Notre-
Dame for the rest of her life! I must try to find her."

He went every day to the church to look for her,
but he never saw her. He tried to find Quasimodo,
but the hunchback never came down from the towers
when Gringoire was there. Claude Frollo, too,
seemed to have disappeared.

In his sleep, Gringoire often saw Esmeralda in
the arms of the hunchback, and then he shouted and
woke up. He left his bed, and said to himself:

"After such a terrible dream as that, I won't be
able to sleep again tonight. I'll go and walk in the
streets until morning." He walked through the dark,
silent city. Without thinking where he was going he
made his way to Notre-Dame.

"Fate must have led me here!" he whispered when he found that he was outside the church; "I know I shall find her now!" He hurried up the steps to the big doors; but they were shut tight, and he could not move them. Suddenly a voice spoke in his ear:

"Leave the doors alone tonight, my old friend!"

A strong hand held Gringoire by the arm, and he shook with fear as he looked into the dark to see whom the hand belonged to.

"You'll never be a good thief until you can see in a night as black as coal!" said the man, with a quiet laugh.

"Who are you?" cried Gringoire.

"Your king!" said the man, and he pushed his face towards Gringoire's; "can you see me now, you poet?"

"Yes—yes, I can," said Gringoire. It was the King of the Beggars. The teeth in his gipsy face shone white as he laughed at the frightened poet.

"Are you seeking your beautiful wife?" the King asked him.

"Yes, I am," Gringoire replied in a whisper. "Can you tell me where she is?"

"You won't find her tonight," said the King, "although I do know where she is. . . . Come with me now and I'll tell you my plan." He hurried down the steps, still holding Gringoire by the arm.

They walked in silence through the streets until they came to the bridge of Saint Michel. The King of the Beggars led Gringoire to the edge of the water.

"This is a good, quiet place to talk in," he said. "I don't like to speak about my plans where other people can listen; especially when my plans are to steal things from a church as famous as Notre-Dame."

"Steal from Notre-Dame!" whispered Gringoire with great surprise.

"It is rich in gold and jewels and money," said the King of the Beggars; "all the things which my people and I like. Besides," he continued, "Esmeralda is there, and we want her to come back to us don't we?"

"Yes, yes!" cried Gringoire.

"We'll bring her out of Notre-Dame tomorrow night," said the King, "and we'll bring enough gold, too, to keep us in comfort for the rest of our lives!"

Seventeen

NOISES IN THE NIGHT

The next night there were no clouds in the sky, and the moon shone. It lit up the dark floor of Notre-Dame with a blue colour like the sea: Esmeralda was walking there, and Djali stepped beside her. Her movements were very quiet, but the golden feet of the goat made a sharp noise on the stone floor. No other sounds broke the silence.

Quasimodo stood in the shadows and watched her as she walked up and down the church. Sometimes she stopped, picked up her goat in her arms and kissed it.

"Isn't the church beautiful at night, Djali?" she whispered. "It is so quiet and calm that sometimes I think I would be happy to live here for ever." She put down the goat and began to walk again.

"But sometimes I wish that I could go out into the city, and be free to live in my own way," she said.

She stood still, lost in thought.

"It seems many years since I sang in the streets, doesn't it, Djali? I wonder if I still remember how to dance! Do you think I can remember, my dear little friend? Shall I try?" She began to sing and to move her feet gently on the cold, stone floor of the empty church.

Her voice sounded thin and sweet in the great building, and she looked very small as she danced alone. She smiled with pleasure while she moved in the way she remembered so well. The hunchback stood in the shadows with his great mouth open. He forgot everything in the joy of her graceful dance, and he began to jump up and down with delight. The girl turned round faster and faster, and the goat began to move its golden feet too. Quasimodo felt so happy that he laughed aloud. He could not hear his own voice, but his strange laugh, like the noise of a rough animal, rang through the empty church.

The girl stopped, but she was not frightened. She knew the voice of Quasimodo so well now that it caused her no pain. She looked round, with a smile, and saw where he was standing. Then she ran to him, held her arms out to show that she was pleased to see him, and took him by the hand. Djali ran after her, and lay down at her feet.

"Come!" she said, and she drew him into the centre of the church; "I will dance a special dance for my dear, kind bell-ringer!"

His face was full of happiness as she began to sing and dance again.

Suddenly there was a deep, loud noise outside the great doors of the church. Esmeralda was too busy with her song and her dance to notice the noise at first, but in a moment she did hear it. She stood still, and turned her frightened eyes to Quasimodo. He could not understand why she had stopped, because he could not hear the noise although it grew louder and louder every minute: it sounded as if many people were trying to break the doors.

"Why will you not continue your beautiful dance?" he asked. "What have I done to frighten you? What is it?"

She pointed to the doors, and made signs to tell him what she could hear.

"Come with me!" he shouted, as soon as he understood. "I don't know who it is, but I shall keep you safe. Have no fear!" He held her hand and ran with her to the foot of the tower and up the stairs to her room. The goat followed close behind them.

"Stay in there until I come back to you," he shouted; then he ran out onto the roof and looked down into the square below.

It was full of people with lights, and there were more people on the steps of Notre-Dame. They were trying to break down the doors with a long, thick piece of wood, a great tree. Time after time they ran at the doors. The doors were very strong, and covered with metal, but they would not be able to stand against the men with the tree for ever. Again and again the men ran up the steps and struck the doors with the tree.

"They aren't soldiers," Quasimodo said to himself, as he watched. "Who can they be? They look very poor and rough. I must hide my dear one from them!" He ran back to Esmeralda.

"I don't know who they are or what they want," he said to her, as she sat on the bed, holding her goat close to her in fear. "But I shall keep you safe, even if I die!"

He took a key from his pocket.

"There is only one other key to your door," he said, "and that is kept by my master. I must shut you in and take this key with me. As soon as I am sure that there is no one in the church who will harm you, I will come back and open the door. You will be safe until I return." His face was full of anxiety as he spoke, but he tried to smile as he left her.

Esmeralda heard the key turn in the door, and she held Djali close to her.

"What will happen to us now? What will happen?" she whispered, and she shut her eyes.

During the day, men worked to repair the roof of Notre-Dame. They went home when the light faded, but they left their instruments behind in the tower. Quasimodo ran along the roof to the place where they kept their materials: he found a heap of big stones, a lot of long pieces of metal—soft, heavy metal. It was *lead*. There was also an iron basket in which the men made a fire. They heated the lead on the fire and poured the liquid metal into the holes in the roof.

"This is what I need!" cried Quasimodo, and he laughed as he picked up the nearest stone. It was so heavy that, although he was as strong as three men, he could only just lift it in both his big hands.

He held it high over his head, went to the edge of the roof and dropped the stone down onto the crowd below. He did not wait to see what happened down there, but he ran back for another big stone, and threw it down too. Another followed, and then another and another. After that he stopped, and looked down to see if he had been successful.

The crowd was further away: the steps were empty, except for some bodies lying as if they were dead. The tree was on the ground, but twenty men ran out of the crowd, picked it up and ran back with it away from the steps.

"Now I'll make it feel warm!" shouted Quasimodo. He went and lit the workmen's fire.

In a few moments, smoke rose into the air: the fire in the iron basket began to burn brightly, and the hunchback fed it with large pieces of wood. Then he hung a big pot full of lead over the fire.

In the square below, a man with a long sword in his hand pointed to the roof and shouted:

"Look! It's burning! The roof is burning!"

"Come on, men!" cried the King of Beggars.

" Fire has come from heaven to help us! God wants to destroy the church! Come on! "

The men with the tree ran forward to the steps, and rushed against the doors. The wood of the doors began to crack: but the iron was only scratched.

" Again! " shouted the men, " we'll charge it again! " and they hurried back down the steps, getting ready to run at the doors again.

Suddenly a great rock fell down into the middle of the tree: it knocked it from their hands, and hit one man and killed him at once. Three other men fell under the tree, and their legs were broken. The shouts were terrible.

Another big stone fell onto the crowd, and the men who could still move ran away.

" Be brave, my good fellows! " cried the King. " We can't be beaten by a few stones! Come on again! " With a shout the men followed him up the steps and drove the tree again and again against the doors.

" The cracks are getting bigger! " cried the men who held the front of the tree. " Now! Again! " and they ran through the stones that fell, one after another, from above.

As soon as one man was hit, another took his place and held the tree, while other men pulled the body out of the way. The square was full of beggars and thieves.

" It's opening! It's opening! " shouted a little fellow standing near the doors. " Three more blows, and we'll be able to get in! "

"One!"

The hole in the wood of the left door was nearly wide enough for a child to get through.

"Two!" The iron across the hole broke with a loud noise, and the crowd shouted.

No stones fell, and the men with the tree rushed at the doors with all their strength.

"Think of the gold, my people!" shouted the King. "It will all be ours!"

"Three!"

The men ran up the steps with the tree, hit the doors with one great, last blow. The hole was big enough for a man to go through. But before anyone could do so, there was a terrible shout of pain from the men who were nearest to the doors.

Hot lead poured down on their heads. It came through the mouths of the stone gargoyles made to carry rain off the roof. The men fell, crying out with pain, and those who could not escape died under the stream of boiling metal. The crowd ran back down the steps, as more and more melted lead poured down from the gargoyles.

The hunchback could be seen, a black shape moving in front of the fire on the roof. The crowd cursed him, but he could not hear.

"There's enough melted lead to keep them out for a few minutes," he said. "Now I'll run and call the soldiers!"

He rushed off the roof and along a passage to the rope of the great bell. With a jump he threw himself onto the rope and pulled it. The bell began to swing, and its noise rang out through the night. Quasimodo laughed aloud.

"That's the music to bring the soldiers!" he cried. He let go of the rope.

"Now for some more hot lead!" he shouted madly as he ran back to the fire on the roof.

"What's that?" he cried, and he stopped in fright on his way up the tower. He shook his head, not sure whether his ears played a trick on him. It was the sharp sound of a whistle, and it ran through his head like a sword.

With a shout of alarm he rushed up to the room where he had left Esmeralda: she needed his help!

Again through the door of her room came the sound of the whistle.

Quasimodo didn't waste a moment: he threw himself against the door and broke it in at once.

He rushed into the little room. Frollo, the priest, was standing beside the bed. He turned from the girl as the hunchback entered. Esmeralda, as white as snow, lay between them, holding Djali against her. The whistle fell from the girl's lips as Quasimodo came in. Her eyes were wide with fear but not as wild as those of the priest, whose eyes burned with desire.

Quasimodo did not look at Frollo. He pushed him aside, knelt down on the bed and took the frightened girl in his arms.

"You are safe now!" he cried, "you are safe with me!"

She closed her eyes and gave a little cry of joy.

"Did he hurt you?" Quasimodo asked her. "Did he touch you?"

"No, no!" she whispered. "I called you as soon as he came. I am all right."

Quasimodo could not hear what she said, but he read her white face like a book. Now he looked up at the priest, standing there as if he were made of wood. Suddenly Frollo, with a strange cry, rushed past the hunchback and ran along the passage onto the roof.

Quasimodo stood up slowly.

"I will come back," he said. "You can trust me." He followed the priest: his movements were full of slow, terrible power.

Eighteen

THE LOST AND FOUND

When the hot lead stopped pouring out of the gargoyles onto the steps of Notre-Dame, the frightened thieves found their courage again.

"Now, my men, there's nothing between us and the gold!" shouted the gipsy King. "Follow me!"

He waved his sword over his head and led the way to the steps, where there was a narrow path through the melted metal.

"On, to the gold!" shouted the crowd, and they followed him into Notre-Dame. Gringoire was among the first to enter.

At that moment there was a cry from the back of the crowd.

"The soldiers are here! The soldiers!" The guard rode into the square: the bell had called them, as Quasimodo hoped it would.

The soldiers struck to right and left with their swords, and many thieves fell under the horses' feet. Blood flowed: cries of terror and anger filled the square.

Inside the church, the King shouted:

"Let's take what we can, men!" and he ran to the gold plates and cups shining in the light of the thieves' lamps. The gold drove out of his mind his wish to carry the gipsy dancer from the church.

"It's all ours, all this gold!" cried the men, and they picked up everything that they could carry. "Quick! It's all ours!"

"I don't like this," Gringoire said to himself. "If I stay there I shall be caught as a thief. This isn't a good time to look for my wife: I'll try to get out another way!" He ran to the end of the church away from the square.

"There's a little door on this side, I remember," he said, and he hurried to the place. "Yes, here it is!"

The door was shut tight with iron bars: Gringoire pulled them aside with all his strength. They opened!

The sky was beginning to show signs of daylight as he ran out of Notre-Dame into the street.

When Quasimodo left Esmeralda on the bed she stayed there for some minutes holding Djali close to her for comfort. She listened to the strange noises that filled the church, and wondered what those sounds were. At last she got up, went to the door of her room and looked down the stairs. Shadows moved about her—shadows thrown by light from the lamps which the thieves were carrying down below.

"I think we must go back to our room, Djali," she said. But at that moment a terrible cry sounded from a window which looked out onto the roof, close to her head.

"What is that?" she cried; "who is it?"

The cry continued for a long time, and then it died away. But the goat did not wait for it to finish: the frightened animal ran away from Esmeralda, and rushed down the stairs.

"Djali!" shouted the gipsy; "Djali, come back, come back to me!" The girl did not think for a moment about her own danger, but she followed her goat down the stairs.

The stairs from the tower into the church came to an end near the little door through which Gringoire had gone: he had left it open behind him. Esmeralda arrived at the bottom of the stairs in the church in time to see Djali run out of the door. She followed.

"Djali!" she called, "Djali!"

The thieves in the church were all too busy to notice the girl as she ran across from the tower and out into the street. No one saw her go.

As she ran down the street, she heard above her head the terrible cry begin again, but she did not wait to look up.

The cry came from the lips of Frollo, his lips

white with fear. When he left the gipsy's room, he felt as if he was burning. He sought air, the cool air of the dying night: he saw an open door and the sky beyond it, and rushed onto the roof. He lay there, breathing heavily.

Then he heard the hunchback come behind him. He pulled himself upright and began to run along the roof: his foot struck against a piece of stone and he fell, outwards from the roof. He caught at the neck of one of the gargoyles, and held onto it with both his hands. He hung above the street, and, as he looked down at the roofs far away below him, he continued to shout at the top of his voice.

Then he looked up. Above him stood the hunchback. Quasimodo's face seemed to be without any expression, as he watched the priest.

"Help me!" cried Frollo.

Quasimodo did not move.

"Help me, for the love of God!" the priest cried again.

The hunchback had only to hold out his hand and he could save the priest with one strong pull: but Quasimodo stood with his arms by his side. He did not speak; he did nothing. He waited for the priest to fall to his death.

The priest looked down again at the street far below him, and again he began to shout. Then he raised his head, and bit his shaking lips until blood flowed from them. His strength was going. He could not hang on for many moments.

And still the hunchback stood and watched him suffer.

The white fingers round the neck of the gargoyle began to lose their hold.

When Gringoire left Notre-Dame he hurried down the narrow street, and then he stopped to think.

"I must keep away from the soldiers," he said, "—and I must keep away from the thieves with their gold. If I walk quietly, alone, I shall be all right."

He was just going to move when he saw a white animal run down the street towards him.

"That's Djali!" he cried when he saw the golden horns of the goat. "Djali, come here, come here!" But the frightened goat ran past him.

Gringoire turned to follow the goat when Esmeralda, with her black hair flying, ran past him too.

"Stop!" he cried, "stop! stop!" and he ran alongside beside her.

She did not turn to see who it was: all her thoughts were for Djali. She had no idea where she was going, and neither had Gringoire. They both followed where the goat led them, down the little streets.

"Esmeralda!" he shouted at her, "my wife!" Still she did not seem to hear him. "Esmeralda! Esmeralda!"

They turned a corner, and there was a crowd of men. Two of them were holding Djali. The others were attacking a little building with all sorts of sharp and heavy instruments. Parts of it already lay in ruins.

"It's Esmeralda! " cried the men who had caught Djali, "it's our own beautiful dancer! " They were thieves and so were the other men with them; she used to live among them. "Esmeralda! " they shouted.

Then the gipsy saw where she was: she was standing beside the Rat-Hole, and the thieves were knocking it to pieces. From inside the low broken walls, which were all that remained of the building, Sister Gudule shouted:

"Leave me alone, leave me alone! "

"What has she done? " asked Esmeralda. "Why are you breaking her home? "

"She cursed us," said the bigger of the two thieves. "She always curses us. We want to teach her a lesson."

"That's right! " shouted a small man with a lamp, "we'll soon make her learn! " His voice was thick with wine.

"Poor old woman, let me come to her! " cried the girl and she pushed between the men.

Sister Gudule was on the floor, like a beaten animal. She was holding something hidden in her hands, and again and again she shouted:

"Leave me alone! Leave me alone! Leave me alone! "

Esmeralda knelt beside her. "They shall not hurt you," she cried. "I won't let them hurt you. Don't be afraid! " She put her arms round the shoulders of the old woman, and for the first time Sister Gudule noticed that the girl was there. In the cold light of the early morning, between the fading lamps of the thieves, she looked up at Esmeralda.

"Who are you?" she cried. "I know you! You look like a gipsy! You . . ."

Suddenly her voice died away: something dropped from her hands, and she fell on the ground and began to search for it.

"Here it is! It is safe!" she cried, and she held up a little baby's shoe.

"Let me see that shoe!" cried Esmeralda. "I must see it!"

And at the same time the girl opened the little green bag with green glass on it, which she wore around her neck. Out of the bag she took a little shoe which was exactly like the other. On it was a piece of paper with these words written in faded ink:

"When you see the other shoe
You will see your mother."

Quickly the old woman put the two shoes together and examined them: she read the paper, and looked up at Esmeralda:

"My daughter!" she cried, "my daughter!"

Esmeralda took her mother in her arms, and kissed her again and again, while the old woman whispered:

"My child! I have found my child!"

"Hurry away!" cried the tall thief who had caught Djali. "Hurry away, before the soldiers arrive." He lifted Esmeralda to her feet. "We'll keep you safe with us," he said.

"Yes, we'll look after you," said the other thieves.

Out of the bag Esmeralda took a little shoe

" I can't leave my mother," cried Esmeralda.

"We'll keep her safe too, won't we, men?" he said. "You'll both be all right with us, if you come quickly!"

After Frollo fell to his death in the street under the tower, Quasimodo slowly returned to Esmeralda's room. When he saw that it was empty he lay on the bed and cried like a child. At last he got up and went to the window.

The sun rose and the city awoke. He looked and looked, as if he sought the beautiful gipsy who was hidden in the city below him. Then his eye was turned, by chance, towards the empty, broken Rat-Hole: but the deserted remains of it were too far away for him to be able to see them. He stood for hours, like one of the gargoyles who always watch, day and night, from the towers of Notre-Dame.

When the light of the winter's day began to fade, he slowly went inside. After a little time one of the bells of Notre-Dame began to ring with a strange, sad music which continued far into the night.

QUESTIONS

1.
1. What did Gringoire want to buy?
2. What was the name of the cold city?
3. What was the name of the square?
4. Who danced between the crowd and the fire?

1. What colour were the dancer's eyes?
2. What were on the little drum?
3. What did the dancer pick up from the ground?
4. What did Sister Gudule hate?

1. How old was the man? "Not more than . . . years old."
2. What colour was the little goat?
3. What did it wear round its neck?
4. How many times did Djali hit the drum?
5. An evil voice in the crowd said it was "all done by . . ." What?

1. What did the goat wave in the air in a funny way?
2. What did the gipsy collect on her drum?
3. How did Gringoire feel when the pretty girl stood in front of him?
4. What did the children run away to find?

1. What has made Sister Gudule ugly?
2. Whose shoe was in the Rat-Hole?
3. Who was singing the song?
4. What did the biggest girl carry?

1. What did the angry crowd begin to move towards?
2. What did the children eat quickly?
3. Who were the men and women carrying?

2.
1. Who went into the church?
2. What did the farmer have on a rope?
3. What colour was the hair round the face?
4. "We must carry our High Priest through . . ." Where?

1. Where were the bells which Quasimodo rang?
2. What was the name of the nasty young man?
3. Where did Quasimodo throw the young man?
4. Who were pleased with the hunchback?
5. What did the beggars push into Quasimodo's hands?

1. Where was the child lying?
2. "This little boy was already . . ." How old?
3. What was the name of the young, important priest?
4. What did the women do when they noticed the priest?

1. What sort of people must we love, as well as the beautiful ones?
2. What did the child stop doing when Frollo picked him up?
3. What ruined Quasimodo's ears?
4. What was the name of the great bell?
5. How many bells had Quasimodo to love?

1. What did Quasimodo touch Marie with?
2. What did the whole tower do when the bells began to ring?
3. What did Quasimodo hang onto?
4. Who often stopped in the streets?

1. What did Quasimodo do as he saw more people coming across the square?
2. Who pulled the crown from Quasimodo's head?
3. What did Quasimodo make cries like?

3.
1. Where were the people, who walked past Gringoire, on their way to?
2. Who was walking down a narrow street in front of Gringoire?
3. Who stepped into the brightly lit doorway of an inn?
4. How many poor men did they pass?

1. What was being made for the next morning?
2. What shone at the far end of the street?
3. What was one of the men dressed in?
4. Quasimodo carried the girl away " as easily as if she were a . . ." What?

1. What did the soldiers make round Quasimodo?
2. Who ran away and disappeared up the street?
3. What did Esmeralda ask the captain?
4. What did Gringoire lie under?
5. What did Gringoire touch?

1. Who were shouting?
2. What did Gringoire pick up?
3. What did Gringoire open his mouth wide to drink?
4. Who did Gringoire see coming towards him out of the dark?

1. What did the second beggar pull himself along with?
2. The blind man " ran faster than . . ." What?
3. Where did Gringoire suddenly find that he was?
4. Who were playing cards?

1. What did Gringoire think was burning?
2. What did the beggars scratch Gringoire with?
3. Who did Gringoire pray to?

4.
1. What were some of the men cleaning from their eyes?
2. What was a child hitting a tin pot with?
3. What colour was the dog?
4. The King said that one of Gringoire's plays " was . . . , very . . ." What?

1. What did a child throw into the fire?
2. What did Gringoire agree to march under?
3. What was the name of " our little man "?
4. What did the men hang from the third piece of wood?

1. What colour was the figure clothed in?
2. What did the King push towards an old chair?
3. What was the money hidden in?
4. " The brass bells looked like angry . . ." What?

1. Gringoire, to stop himself, " caught hold of . . ." What?
2. Which word died on Gringoire's lips?
3. What did the King push with his foot?
4. What did the King lift in the air?
5. " You must either marry one of our women, or marry our . . ." What?

1. Who did not like the look of Gringoire?
2. What shape was the face of the large young woman?
3. Who followed Esmeralda?

    4. What did the King take from the table?

    5. How many pieces did the cup break into?

5.   . 1. Where did Esmeralda bring things from?

    2. Esmeralda escaped from Gringoire's arm " Like a . . ." What?

    3. What did Gringoire bite?

    1. What was in the jug?

    2. How many apples were left when Gringoire's first hunger was satisfied?

    3. What did Esmeralda break?

    4. Esmeralda said that she would, perhaps, have Gringoire for her . . . What?

    5. Esmeralda said that love " is to be two and yet to be . . ." What?

    1. What did Gringoire do as he remembered how little he had helped Esmeralda?

    2. What did the small bag hang on?

    3. What colour was the piece of glass?

    4. What sort of power did Esmeralda say the bag had?

    5. What flew out of the gate?

    1. What did Gringoire blow on?

    2. Who taught Gringoire?

    3. What did Gringoire want to be?

    4. What couldn't Gringoire get enough of?

    5. What did Gringoire lie down on?

6.   1. What had the judge had the night before?

    2. What did the judge have to listen to that day?

    3. How long was the hunchback first ordered to be beaten for?

    4. What colour did the judge's face turn?

    5. What did the judge go on to?

    1. What were the wrongdoers tied to?

    2. The crowds' " hearts were turned to . . ." What?

    3. Whose eyes " shone with a mad light "?

    4. Who joined the crowd round the Wheel?

    5. What did the ropes cut through?

    1. What did they tie Quasimodo down with?

    2. What did the torturer put beside the Wheel?

    3. What were on the ends of the ropes?

    4. What was Quasimodo's eye bright with?

    5. What did the torturer try as hard as he could to do?

    1. What colour was the officer's horse?

    2. What did two soldiers cover Quasimodo's back with?

    3. What did the priest ride on?

    4. When Frollo saw who the man on the Wheel was, "he quickly looked at . . ." What?

    1. What did Quasimodo's strange voice sound like?

    2. What did a man pick up from the dirty street?

    3. What did Esmeralda have in her hand?

    4. What did the crowd now feel?

7.   1. Who had the girls come to visit?

    2. Who smiled at Fleur and Captain Phoebus?

    3. Phoebus knew the gipsy " by her . . ." What?

4. Who was Alice holding?
1. Who pointed at the man in black?
2. Who was the man in black looking at?
3. Where did Phoebus put his head?
4. Esmeralda's " face became as red as a . . ." What?
1. Who " was the first to break the uncomfortable silence "?
2. Fleur said that Esmeralda had " a good . . ." What?
3. Who did Esmeralda say she was sorry for?
1. What colour were Esmeralda's arms?
2. " It is not the dress that matters, but the . . ." What?
3. What did the goat catch its horns in?
4. What did Fleur notice hanging round the goat's neck?
5. What did Fleur very much want to know?
1. What did Djali finish while Monique emptied the bag?
2. What did Djali push the letters with?
3. Where did Fleur hide her face?
4. Which girl did Phoebus follow?

8.
1. What did Claude Frollo have in the north tower?
2. Who did Frollo pass on his way down the stairs?
3. What was tied to the chair?
4. What was the man trying to win from the crowd?
1. How many women did the cat scratch?
2. Who followed Gringoire into Notre-Dame?
3. Gringoire spoke " about the broken . . ." What?
1. Who would kill any man who tried to make love to Esmeralda?
2. What " burned into " Esmeralda's memory " when the hunchback tried to carry her away "?
3. " I tell her it's all a . . ." What?
4. How many months did Esmeralda take to teach Djali to spell ' Phoebus '?
1. What did Esmeralda often repeat to herself?
2. " The gipsies seem to think that the sun is their . . ." What?
3. What did the priest seize " the surprised Gringoire " by?

9.
1. What was Frollo's mind filled with thoughts of?
2. " The words became louder and louder, until the priest was . . ." What?
3. What did Frollo pick up?
4. " Stars shone clear, like . . ." What?
1. What did Frollo hide in?
2. What was the servant just about to do when she saw Frollo?
3. Where did the servant tell her story to Frollo?
4. " She spoke of Captain Phoebus with . . ." What?
1. What did the servant always say that Captain Phoebus was?
2. What was the woman called?
3. Frollo's " hand was hot on . . ." What?

10.
1. What did the old woman do as she slowly walked?
2. What was the old woman's thin voice like?
3. What did Phoebus give to the old woman?
4. What was still on the stick?
5. What did the boy think he was?
1. What did the window of the room look out over?

2. " Something darker than the clouds covered the face of the moon." What?
3. " I have long dreamed of a . . ." What?
1. Phoebus called Esmeralda a foolish . . . What?
2. Phoebus " now spoke his words like . . ." What?
3. What did Phoebus steal?
4. Who love to see the lions?
1. What did Esmeralda ask Phoebus to teach her about?
2. What did Phoebus pretend to look at?
3. Esmeralda asked Phoebus: " Why do you speak as if you were my . . ." What?
1. Esmeralda " raised her eyes towards the . . . and the . . ." What?
2. What did Esmeralda see descend upon Phoebus?
3. Who did Esmeralda see standing all round her?
4. Esmeralda " heard, as in a dream, a voice say . . ." What?

11.
1. Who did Gringoire go to?
2. " I'll start tonight, this . . ." What?
3. Who did Gringoire follow?
4. Whose ugly voice did Gringoire begin to listen to?
1. Where was the knife stuck?
2. What was " all over the floor "?
3. What did the old woman want some money to buy?
4. " A goat is often a friend of a . . ." What?
1. What colour were Esmeralda's lips?
2. What made a cruel sound?
3. What came through the little door?
4. What did the priest take from the table?
1. What was the time?
2. " The people were sure that the . . . was a . . ." What?
3. Who shook Esmeralda by the arm?
4. " My Phoebus! This is worse than . . ." What?
1. What sort of voice did Esmeralda answer in?
2. The priest demanded that Esmeralda should be . . . What?
3. When Esmeralda disappeared, where did a cry come from?

12.
1. " It was dark, except for . . ." What?
2. Who sat on a black, wooden bed?
3. What colour were the officer's clothes?
4. What did the torturer hold up in both his hands?
1. What did the torturer prepare to turn?
2. Who " died five minutes ago "?
3. Who " cursed quietly "?
4. Who had almost to carry Esmeralda out of the door?

13.
1. Why couldn't the prisoners tell day from night?
2. What was a man holding?
3. What did Esmeralda slowly rub?
4. What did Esmeralda begin to weep like?
1. What did the priest's hand feel like on her skin?
2. What did Claude Frollo hold close to his face?
3. Frollo said that before he saw Esmeralda he was . . . What?
1. Where did Frollo kneel?
2. " We can live together in some little . . ." What?

3. What did Esmeralda repeat again and again?

14. 1. What "hasn't come round the corner"?
2. The soldier told Sister Gudule to mind her . . . What?
3. What did the soldiers carry?
4. What did Sister Gudule hold?
1. What was the colour of Esmeralda's dress?
2. What would the hangman soon cut off?
3. "She doesn't look as if she could murder a . . ." What?
4. What did the soldier push between the bars of the window?
5. What did Sister Gudule do when she let go of the bars?
1. The cry of what came from the cart?
2. What sort of music flowed out into the square?
3. What did the line of priests move like?
4. What did the hunchback hold?
5. What flew past the hunchback?
1. How many men untied the ropes from Esmeralda and Djali?
2. What did the voices of the priests praying together sound like?
3. What did the hunchback do to the two men who held Esmeralda?
4. In a church, what is everybody safe from?
5. What was Quasimodo's big, bushy head like?
1. What did Quasimodo's eye fill with?
2. "He had beaten the power of their Law with the power of his . . ." What?
3. Quasimodo carried the gipsy "as if she were as light as . . ." What?
4. What did the great, happy cry shake?

15. 1. What did Esmeralda see below when she half opened her eyes?
2. Where did Quasimodo lay Esmeralda?
3. What had a kind woman left at the door of Notre-Dame?
4. What did Quasimodo put over his eye?
5. Whose food had the hunchback brought Esmeralda?
1. Where did the low door of Esmeralda's room open onto?
2. What did Esmeralda cover Djali's head with?
3. At night, what did Esmeralda walk all round?
1. What did Esmeralda see at the window?
2. What did Quasimodo hide behind?
3. When Quasimodo "saw that she tried to draw him to her, his whole face . . ." What?
1. What was the saddest thing in the world?
2. Where did Quasimodo take a whistle from?
3. Where did Quasimodo lay the whistle?

16. 1. What helped to heal Esmeralda's wounded thoughts?
2. What did Esmeralda like best of all?
3. What did Quasimodo want to be like?
4. Where did the old song come from?
5. What did Esmeralda do at the sight of Quasimodo's ugly face?
1. What did Quasimodo seem like among the gargoyles?
2. Quasimodo asked why he was not made of . . . What?

3. What did Esmeralda begin to forget?
1. Where did the priest hide when Esmeralda walked in the church at night?
2. What made Frollo very angry?
3. Gringoire said: "I must try to . . ." What?
4. When did Gringoire go to the church to look for Esmeralda?
1. Where did Gringoire make his way to without thinking?
2. "You'll never be a good thief until . . ." What?
3. The King said he knew where . . . What?
1. What was the name of the bridge?
2. Where did the King plan to steal things from?
3. When did the King plan to bring Esmeralda out of Notre-Dame?

17.
1. What colour was the floor in the moonlight?
2. Who stepped beside Esmeralda?
3. Who stood in the shadows?
4. What " rang through the empty church "?
1. " Djali ran after her, and . . ." What?
2. What did Esmeralda point to?
3. Who followed close behind Quasimodo and Esmeralda?
4. What were the doors covered with?
1. What did Esmeralda sit on?
2. What did Quasimodo take from his pocket?
3. What did Quasimodo try to do as he left Esmeralda?
1. What did Quasimodo find a heap of?
2. How many men ran out of the crowd?
3. What did Quasimodo hang over the fire?
4. What was only scratched?
1. What suddenly fell down into the middle of the tree?
2. " The square was full of beggars and . . ." What?
3. " Think of the . . ." What?
4. Which men gave " a terrible shout of pain "?
1. What did hot lead pour through?
2. " Now I'll run and call the . . ." What?
3. What began to swing?
1. What ran through Quasimodo's head like a sword?
2. What did Quasimodo throw himself against?
3. Whose eyes " burned with terrible pain "?
4. What did Quasimodo take in his arms?
5. Where did Frollo run?

18.
1. What did the gipsy King wave over his head?
2. Who rode into the square?
3. What did Gringoire pull " aside with all his strength "?
4. What was the sky beginning to show signs of?
1. Who were carrying the lamps?
2. Where did " a terrible cry " sound from?
3. Who were too busy to notice the girl?
4. What did Esmeralda hear above her head as she rushed down the street?
1. What did Frollo hit his foot against?
2. What did Frollo hold onto " with both his hands "?
3. What did Frollo bite?

1. " I must keep away from the . . . with their . . ." What?
2. What did Gringoire see running down the street towards him?
3. How many men were holding Djali?
4. Who were the men?
1. Esmeralda " was standing beside . . ." What?
2. " His voice was thick with . . ." What?
3. What dropped from Sister Gudule's hands?
4. What did the girl open?
5. What were the words written in?
1. What did the old woman whisper?
2. " You'll be all right with us, if you . . ." What?
3. How long did Quasimodo stand " like one of the gargoyles "?

LIST OF EXTRA WORDS

deaf, 2

gargoyle, 14
gibbet, 1
gipsy, 1

horns, 5
hour-glass, 6
hunchback, 2

lead (metal), 17

pillar, 14
pillory, 6

torture, 6